Nicola
and the
Viscount

Meg Cabot

MACMILLAN CHILDREN'S BOOKS

First published 2002 by Avon True Romance
a trademark of HarperCollins *Publishers*, USA

This edition published 2002 by Macmillan Children's Books
a division of Macmillan Publishers Limited
20 New Wharf Road, London N1 9RR
Basingstoke and Oxford
www.panmacmillan.com

Associated companies throughout the world

ISBN 0 330 41517 4

9 8

A CIP catalogue record for this book is available from
the British Library.

Typeset by Intype London Ltd
Printed and bound in Great Britain by
Mackays of Chatham plc, Chatham, Kent

For Benjamin

Many thanks to Beth Ader, Jennifer Brown, Laura Langlie, Abby McAden and David Walton.

Part 1

Part I

One

London, 1808

'Oh, Nicky.' The Honourable Miss Eleanor Sheridan sighed. 'I would give anything to be an orphan, like you. You are *so* lucky.'

Miss Nicola Sparks, far from taking offence at her friend's remark, looked thoughtfully at her own reflection in the great gilt-framed mirror before them. 'Aren't I, though?' she agreed.

Eleanor's mother let out an indignant harrumph. 'Well, I like that!' the Lady Sheridan said as she handed a pile of Eleanor's undergarments to the girl's French maid to pack. 'I'm terribly sorry your father and I have been so unobliging, Eleanor, in not perishing in a more timely manner.'

Eleanor, who stood behind Nicola at the dressing table, examining her chestnut brown curls in the mirror with the same critical eye Nicola was applying to her glossy black ones, rolled her eyes.

'Oh, don't be tiresome, Mama,' Eleanor said. 'You know I don't wish you and Papa dead. It's only that lucky Nicola gets to pick from a horde of invitations where she'll go now that school's finished, while I have no choice in the matter at all. I've got to spend the rest of my life – until I'm married, in any case – with you and Papa and wretched Nat and Phil.'

'I can arrange for you to spend the rest of your life with your great-aunts in Surrey,' Lady Sheridan pointed out drily, 'if our household is so offensive to you. I am sure they would love to have you.'

Eleanor's hazel eyes widened, and she spun from the dressing table to face her mother. '*Surrey!*' she burst out. 'What in heaven's name would I do in *Surrey*?'

'I'm sure I can't say.' Lady Sheridan closed the first of her daughter's many trunks, then moved to the second. 'But I can promise you'll find out if you don't start showing a little more sense. Nicola, lucky to be an orphan, indeed!'

Nicola, roused by this remark from an examination of her new, upswept coiffure – the first she'd ever been allowed by Martine, her own very strict French maid, who did not believe it was proper for girls younger than sixteen to wear their hair up – turned around on the tasselled stool upon which she sat, and said to her friend's mother with some gravity, 'But I *am* lucky, Lady Sheridan. I mean, it isn't as if I ever actually knew my parents, so you see, I cannot miss them. They died a few months after I was born. And though their deaths were tragic, at least they perished together . . .'

'So romantic,' Eleanor said with a sigh. 'I hope that when I die, it is like Nicky's parents did, drowning in the river Arno after a sudden storm.'

'And though Father hadn't any money to speak of,' Nicola went on calmly, as if Eleanor hadn't spoken, 'he did leave me the abbey, which provides me with some income – not much, of course, but enough for a maid and school and new lace for a bonnet now and then.'

Nicola turned back towards her reflection, which, though by no means the prettiest one at Madame Vieuxvincent's

4

Seminary for Young Ladies – Eleanor surely had the distinction of being the most beautiful girl at school – no one, with the exception perhaps of Nicola herself, would dispute was anything but pleasing. Nicola found the fact that her nose bore traces of a powdering of freckles, left over from an injudicious river expedition the summer before with neither hat nor parasol, a dreadful shortcoming.

Still, freckles notwithstanding, she was forced to admit, 'So really, Lady Sheridan, Eleanor is right. I *am* lucky. At least I have been, up until now. What shall happen to me next . . .' Nicola bit her lower lip, and watched in the mirror as it turned a deep scarlet. Rouge was strictly forbidden at the school – as, unfortunately for Nicola's freckles, was powder – and so the girls were forced to resort to pinches and bites if they hoped to achieve the effect of blooming health, though Nicola, with her ivory complexion and ebony lashes and hair, usually managed quite well without such tricks. 'I haven't the slightest idea. I suppose now that I'm finished with my schooling, I shall be blown about by life, like a thistle in the wind.'

'Well, if you should ever tire of being a thistle,' Lady Sheridan said, shaking out one of her daughter's sadly crumpled shawls before handing it to Eleanor's maid, Mirabelle, to press between sheets of tissue, then fold into the trunk before them, 'you are always welcome to stay with us, Nicola, for as long as you like.'

'As if she would want to,' Eleanor cried, turning away from the sun-filled window she'd gone to stand by before. 'Why, Nicky's had invitations to come and live with some of the richest girls at school! Sophia Dunleavy's asked her. Oh, and Charlotte Murphy. Even Lady Honoria Bartholomew's asked her. *Her* parents have a town house on Park Lane, and Lady Honoria's got her own curricle . . . not to mention an entire wardrobe copied straight from the fashion plates of *La Belle Assemblée*, just for her first season out. And *her* father's an *earl* – the Earl of Farelly – and not a measly viscount, like Papa.'

'Good Lord.' But Lady Sheridan was not, as one might have thought, commenting on the grandness of Lady Honoria Bartholomew's lineage. 'I can't imagine what Lady Farelly could be thinking, inviting a girl like Nicola to stay during her own daughter's first season out. The woman must be mad.'

Nicola, hearing this, felt her eyes suddenly fill with tears. Why, Eleanor had been her most bosom friend through their years together at Madame's! How many holidays had Nicola spent at Sheridan Park? How many weekends had she passed at the Sheridans' London home? She had always rather fancied that kindly, comfortable Lady Sheridan looked upon her as a second daughter.

So why on earth would she ever say such a thing?

'A girl like Nicola?' Eleanor, much to Nicola's gratification, was quick to rush to her friend's defence. 'Why, Mama! What a thing to say! And right in front of Nicky, too!'

But Lady Sheridan only looked annoyed. 'For heaven's sake, Eleanor,' she said in her no-nonsense way. 'I only meant that Lady Farelly must not have the sense God gave a goose to invite a girl as pretty as Nicola to stay at a time when her own daughter – who is no picture, mind you, for all her money – will be angling for a husband.'

Nicola realized that what she'd thought to be an insult of the worst kind had actually turned out to be rather a nice compliment. So she blinked back her tears and, feeling a rush of affection for her friend's mother, leaped from the tasselled stool and ran to embrace her.

'Oh, Lady Sheridan,' Nicola cried, not caring that she'd nearly upset the armful of linens Mirabelle had been carrying. 'You are so wonderful! You almost make me wish I were staying with you, after all.'

Lady Sheridan, looking a bit startled, nevertheless returned Nicola's hug, patting her fondly on the shoulder.

'You are a sweet girl, Nicola,' Lady Sheridan admitted. 'I think you've done a world of good for Eleanor. Lord knows we chose boarding school for her only as a last resort. All those governesses we hired despaired of her ever grasping even a basic knowledge of French and petit point. But thanks to you – and Madame, of course – she's grown a good bit less silly. I believe it was because of your influence that she finally put her mind to her studies.'

'*Mama!*' Eleanor protested. 'I am hardly silly. Why, I received better marks than anyone in the entire school this term, with the exception of Nicola. And I read the whole of *The Lay of the Minstrel* only last month.' But she was soon distracted by a noise outside her bedchamber window, and quickly forgot her outrage in her eagerness to report, 'Oh, look, Nicky! It's *him*! The God himself! He *did* come, after all, just as Lady Honoria said he would!'

Nicola released Lady Sheridan at once and rushed to the window, nearly snagging her white muslin gown on the edge of one of Eleanor's trunks, and causing Mirabelle to gasp, 'Oh, mademoiselle! Your lovely dress! Have a care!'

Eleanor, making room for Nicola on the window seat, declared scornfully, 'Oh, who cares about a stupid dress when there's a *god* in the carriage drive?'

Lady Sheridan and her daughter's maid exchanged meaningful glances, but Nicola didn't care how flighty they thought her and Eleanor: it was well worth it, considering the sight that awaited them below . . .

'Oh,' Eleanor whispered, so as not to be overheard – for it was, after all, a warm spring day, and all the windows at Madame's had been thrown open to allow the air to circulate as the girls moved out, it being the last day of the school term. 'Look at him, Nicky. Have you ever seen such a vision?'

Nicola had to admit that she had not. At least not since the last time young Lord Sebastian had come to call upon his sister, the Lady Honoria, a fellow boarding student at the seminary.

'He has the veriest golden hair I ever saw,' Eleanor declared in a low voice. 'And look at those shoulders!'

Nicola, gazing down at the tall young man, saw neither the golden hair nor the impressive width of shoulder. Instead she remembered Lord Sebastian's eyes – as blue, she knew, as her own, and her own had been compared by a few of the more imaginative girls to the stone in the sapphire brooch Madame wore on special occasions such as today. Blue as the sky overhead Lord Sebastian Bartholomew's eyes had looked the first time she'd gazed into them . . .

And that had been at the school's last recitation day when Lady Honoria's brother, down from Oxford to visit his only sister, had complimented Nicola after her performance of Walter Scott's *Marmion*.

'Miss Sparks,' Lord Sebastian had said, in a voice as gentle and deep as ever Nicola had imagined Lancelot addressing his fair Guenevere. 'How I envy Lochinvar, if only for having his name formed by so sweet a pair of lips.'

She'd received the compliment without a word, only a curtsy and, she feared, a blush. But how could she have spoken? What could she have said? Eleanor was quite right: the man was like a god, an absolute Apollo, or even an Adonis . . . at least as Apollo and Adonis were depicted by

8

the great masters, copies of which Madame had hanging in the salon for her boarders' edification.

And like Apollo, the sun god, Lord Sebastian seared Nicola's soul. Just a single glance. That was all it took.

Well, had it taken Romeo more than that to seize for ever the heart of his sweet Juliet?

And here Lord Sebastian was again, and this time Nicola was determined to do more than curtsy. No, this time she would impress the God with her wit and poise. See if she didn't.

And she supposed it wouldn't hurt that she looked so very well, with her new upswept coiffure. Why, the last time she'd seen him, she'd been in braids! He must have thought her positively childish! It was too bad about the freckles, but there was nothing, she supposed, to be done about those. At least until she got to London and was able to get her hands on some face powder.

'I wonder if he heard your *Lady of the Lake* at the recitation this morning,' mused Eleanor, watching as Lord Sebastian directed a servant carrying one of his sister's trunks toward their waiting carriage. 'If he did, he must certainly love you now. For no one can hear you recite Scott, Nicky, and not love you.'

Nicola was fervently hoping this was true just as a decidedly unfeminine voice from behind the two girls demanded, 'Who loves Nicky?'

Both Nicola and Eleanor spun around. Then, when they saw who it was, both girls moved instinctively to block the view from the window.

'Nathaniel, what can you be thinking?' Lady Sheridan scolded her eldest son. 'Entering your sister's bedchamber without knocking first! I have never heard of such a thing.'

'The door was open.' Eleanor's older brother, the

Honourable Nathaniel Sheridan, flopped on to a nearby settee and regarded the two girls with a gaze that was as speculative as it was mischievous. 'Who loves Nicky?' he repeated.

Nicola, abashed, flung a look of appeal in Lady Sheridan's direction. Nathaniel Sheridan seemed to delight in mercilessly teasing his sister, as well as Nicola, whenever he happened to see her, which fortunately was not often, since Nathaniel had been, up until recently, busy studying mathematics – in which he had, in fact, successfully gained a first – at Oxford.

But now, his degree secured, Nathaniel had been turned loose upon the world, and Nicola could not help feeling a bit sorry for it . . . the world, that is. Though she secretly suspected that Nathaniel's behaviour would not have been half so infuriating had he not happened to be so very attractive. Oh, he was no Apollo – heaven forbid! No golden-haired, blue-eyed god he.

But he was quite tall, and did happen to have a very charming smile, and the way his brown hair sometimes flopped into his eyes – hazel, like his sister's – Nicola found disarming in the extreme. It was quite intolerable that so irritating a person could be so physically prepossessing.

Nathaniel's disdain for poetry, however, was a very great failing. He had once even had the gall to call the brave and handsome Lochinvar 'that great ass,' a sin for which Nicola knew she could never forgive him.

Fortunately, Lady Sheridan was as disapproving of her eldest son's occasionally waggish treatment of his sister and her friends as Nicola was of his lack of respect for literary beauty.

'You'll be addressing Nicola as Miss Sparks from now on, Nathaniel,' the young man's mother declared. 'As of today, she is no longer in the schoolroom, and you will accord her the courtesy you would if she were a stranger to you, and not Eleanor's particular friend.' To Nicola, Lady Sheridan said, 'But you, my dear, should still feel free to crack him over the head with your parasol if he persists in being irritating.'

Before Nathaniel could protest too much over this, Eleanor's other brother, ten-year-old Phillip, burst into the bedchamber his sister would soon be vacating forever, also without bothering to knock. He had no eyes for his female relations, however. All his attention was focused on his twenty-year-old brother.

'Nat,' he cried excitedly. 'You should see the phaeton that just pulled 'round! Matching bays, eighteen hands each if they're an inch, and had to have cost a hundred quid each, easy—'

'Phillip!' Lady Sheridan was shocked by the lack of decorum her sons were exhibiting. 'Really. A gentleman always knocks before entering a lady's boudoir.'

But her youngest son merely looked confused. 'Lady? What lady? It's only Eleanor's room, after all. Listen, Nat, you must come and see these bays . . . '

'Mademoiselle.' All eyes turned to the doorway, where Nicola's maid Martine stood, holding on to her mistress's bonnet and parasol, her dark eyes wide. 'Begging your pardon, mademoiselle, but the Lady Farelly sent me to fetch you. Their carriage just pulled 'round. They are all waiting for you downstairs.'

'So those are Lord Farelly's bays, then,' Phillip said with a low, appreciative whistle. 'Well, no wonder.'

His elder brother's reaction to this news was not nearly so sanguine, however. Nathaniel nearly leaped from the seat in which he'd been lolling a second before. 'Lord Farelly?' he

11

burst out, not very politely. 'What the devil? You're not going to stay with the *Bartholomews*, are you, Nicky?'

'What if I am?' Nicola wanted to know, as she reached for the bonnet her maid held. 'They are perfectly nice people.'

'Perfectly *rich* people, you mean,' Phillip said. 'No wonder Nicky's staying with them, with bays like that.'

'Phillip!' Lady Sheridan looked to be at the end of her patience with her children. 'It is uncouth to comment upon the financial status of others. And Nathaniel, I told you before, you are to address Nicola as Miss Sparks.'

'And really, Phil,' Eleanor said scornfully. 'The idea of Nicky choosing to stay with the Bartholomews over us simply because they happen to have more money than we do is positively ridiculous. How could you think something so wicked, and of our Nicky? Why, it's got nothing to do with that. The fact is, she's in love with Lord Sebas—'

'Eleanor!' Nicola cried.

But it was too late. The damage was done.

'So *that's* who you were talking about when I walked in.' Nathaniel pushed some dark hair from his eyes and glared at Nicola. 'Well, just so you know, Sebastian Bartholomew is nothing but an *oarsman*.'

Nicola, furious over hearing the God slighted – though she couldn't imagine why joining a college rowing team should be such a crime – but equally furious with Eleanor for letting her most treasured secret slip, gasped. She could not remember ever feeling so truly angry with anyone. Anger, Madame had always reminded her pupils, was unbecoming in a lady. And so Nicola struggled to contain her feelings. But she could not. They burst from her in a frothy torrent.

'You should be ashamed of yourself, saying things like that,' Nicola cried. 'You don't even know him!'

'I know him a good deal better than you do,' Nathaniel replied. 'He was in my same college at Oxford.'

'And?' Nicola demanded. 'So what if he was an oarsman? I should think that's a good deal more exciting than what *you* were doing at Oxford.'

'Getting an education, you mean?' Nathaniel's laugh was humourless. 'Yes, I should say Bartholomew had a more *exciting* time of it at Oxford than I did.'

Though she still wasn't certain what he meant, Nicola felt another spurt of rage. How dare anyone speak disparagingly of the God! She wanted to break something, but since this was Eleanor's room, and not her own, there was nothing nearby that she could get away with breaking, so she settled for stamping a slippered foot and declaring, 'You make him sound like a wastrel!'

'You said it,' Nathaniel retorted. 'Not me.'

'Don't pay any attention to him, Nicky,' Eleanor said. 'Lord Sebastian is a poetry lover, like you. You know how Nat feels about poetry.'

'Nathaniel's feelings about poetry aside,' Lady Sheridan said, stepping between her son and her daughter's friend, who stood almost nose-to-nose, their arms folded across their chests and their breath coming a little too quickly as they glared angrily at one another, 'are you quite certain your uncle approves of your staying with Lord and Lady Farelly, Nicola?'

'My uncle?' Nicola shot Lady Sheridan a bewildered glance.

'The Grouser,' Eleanor prompted helpfully.

Understanding dawning, Nicola cried, 'Oh, you mean Lord Renshaw? But he isn't my uncle, Lady Sheridan, only my cousin . . . and my guardian. And yes, he knows all about it. My staying with the Bartholomews, I mean.' She narrowed her eyes at Nathaniel. 'The Grouser is a bit of a curmudgeon, but at least *he* isn't a narrow-minded poetry hater.'

Nathaniel opened his mouth to comment on this, but his mother said, before he could utter a sound, 'Fine, then. If Nicola's guardian knows and approves, then I don't think, Nathaniel, that we can have any objec—'

'Oh, he doesn't approve,' Eleanor interrupted with a giggle. 'The Grouser was quite put out with Nicky for not agreeing to stay with him and that dreadful milksop of a son of his in London. Wasn't he, Nicky?'

Lady Sheridan looked heavenward. 'Eleanor,' she said. 'Kindly do not refer to Lord Renshaw as the Grouser, and his heir as a milksop.'

Eleanor, surprised, asked, 'Why shouldn't I? He *is* one.'

'Nevertheless—'

'Mademoiselle.' Martine, still standing in the doorway, cleared her throat meaningfully. 'I am sorry to interrupt, but we must not keep Her Ladyship waiting.'

Nicola turned to Lady Sheridan. Really, this was not the way she'd wanted to say goodbye to these people who'd been so kind to her for all the years she and Eleanor had been at school together. Then again, surely they'd see one another quite often, once they were all back in London. She and Eleanor would undoubtedly be invited to many of the same balls and soirées . . .

Unfortunately, it seemed likely Nathaniel would also be there. But Nicola intended to maintain an air of queenly disdain around that person from now on. Imagine, slighting the God in that way!

'I must go,' Nicola said regretfully to Lady Sheridan. 'But might I call upon Eleanor, when she is settled back at home?'

'You may call upon Eleanor any time you like, Nicola,' Lady Sheridan said, reaching out to wrap her daughter's closest friend in her arms. 'And remember, if you should change your mind about staying with the Bartholomews – for *whatever* reason – our home is always open to you.'

Nicola returned the hug gratefully, averting her gaze from Nathaniel, who she saw was still looking at her with a very grim expression on his face. Eleanor's brother was a tease, it was true. But he was also very, very intelligent. Didn't his first in mathematics prove that?

Still, he was wrong, Nicola knew, both about poetry and about Lord Sebastian Bartholomew.

And she'd prove it to him, one way or another.

TWO

Dear Nana,

I hope you received the gifts I sent you. The shawl is pure Chinese silk, and the pipe I sent for Puddy is ivory-handled! You needn't worry about the expense; I was able to use my monthly stipend. I am staying with the Bartholomews – I told you about them in my last letter – and they won't let me spend a penny on myself! Lord Farelly insists on paying for everything. He is such a kind man. He is very interested in locomotives and the railway. He says that some day all of England will be connected by rail, and that one might start out in the morning in Brighton, and at the end of the day find oneself in Edinburgh!

I found that a bit hard to believe, as I'm certain you do, too, but that is what he says.

Nicola paused in her letter writing to read over what she had already written. As she did so, she nibbled thoughtfully on the feathered end of her pen.

Nana was not, of course, her real grandmother. Nicola had no real grandparents, all of them having been carried away by influenza before she was even born. Because her sole remaining relative, Lord Renshaw, had had no interest in nor knowledge of raising a little girl, Nicola had been reared, until she was old enough to go away to school, by the wife of the caretaker of her father's estate, Beckwell Abbey. It was to this woman – and her husband, whom Nicola affectionately referred to as Puddy – that Nicola looked for grandmotherly advice and comfort. Dependent, as Nicola was, on the small income the local farmers supplied by renting the abbey's many rolling fields for their sheep to graze upon, Nana and Puddy lived modestly, but well.

But never so well as Nicola had been living for the past month. The Bartholomews, as it turned out, were every bit as wealthy as Phillip Sheridan had declared . . . perhaps even wealthier.

But what Phillip had not mentioned, since he could not have known, was that the Bartholomews were also generous, almost to a fault. Nicola needed to express only the slightest desire, and her wish was immediately granted. She had learned to bite back exclamations over bonnets or trinkets at the many shops she and Honoria frequented, lest she find herself the owner of whatever it was she'd admired. She could not allow these kind people to keep buying gifts for her . . . especially as she had no way to return the favour.

Besides which, Nicola did not really *need* new gowns or bonnets. Necessity, in the form of her limited income, had forced her to become a skilled and creative seamstress. She had taught herself how to alter an old gown with a new flounce or sleeves until it looked as if it had come straight from a Parisian dress shop. And she was almost as fine a milliner as any in the city, having rendered many an out-of-fashion bonnet stylish in the extreme with an artful addition of a silk rose here, or an artificial cherry there.

Eyeing her letter, Nicola wondered if she ought to add something about the God. It seemed as if it might be a good idea, since it was entirely possible that Sebastian Bartholomew was going to play an important role in all of their lives, if things kept up the way they had been. Having grown up almost completely sheltered from them, Nicola knew very little, it was true, about young men, but it did seem to her that Honoria's brother had been *most* attentive since she'd come to stay. He escorted the girls nearly every-where they went, except when he was not busy with his own friends, who were quite fond of gambling and horses, like most young men – except perhaps Nathaniel Sheridan, who was too concerned with managing his father's many estates ever to stop for a game of whist or bagatelle.

Even more exciting, the God was always the first to ask Nicola for a dance at whatever ball they happened to be attending. Sometimes he even secured *two* dances with her in a single evening. Three dances with a gentlemen to whom she was not engaged, of course, would be scandalous, so that was not even a possibility.

On these occasions Nicola's heart sang, and she could not believe there existed in London a happier soul than she. It seemed incredible, but it appeared she had actually accomplished what she'd set out to do, which was impress the young Viscount Farnsworth – for that was Lord Sebastian's title, which he would hold until his father died, and he assumed the title of Earl of Farelly – with her wit and charm. How she had done it – and quite without the help of any face powder – she could not say, but she did not think she could be mistaken in the signs: the God admired her, at least a little. She supposed her hair, which she wore upswept all the time now, with Martine's aid, had helped. All that Nicola needed to for ever seal her happiness was for the God to propose marriage. If he did – no, when, *when* – she had already decided she would say yes.

But there was, in the back of her mind, a niggling doubt that such a proposal might ever really materialize. She was, after all, not wealthy. She had nothing but her passably pretty face and keen fashion sense to recommend her. Handsome young men of wealth and importance rarely asked penniless girls like Nicola – even penniless girls of good family and excellent education – to marry them. Love matches were all well and good, but, as Madame had often reminded them, starvation is not pleasant. Young men who did not marry as their fathers instructed them often found themselves cut off without a penny. And it was perfectly untrue that one could live on love alone. Love could not, after all, put bread on the table and meat in the larder.

But from parental objections to a match between her and the God, at least, Nicola felt she was safe. Lord and Lady Farelly seemed prodigiously fond of her. Why, in the short time since she'd come to live with them, they seemed already to think of her as a second daughter, including her in all of their family conversations, and even occasionally dropping their formal address of her as Miss Sparks, and calling her Nicola.

No, should Lord Sebastian see fit to propose to her, she could foresee no difficulties from *that* quarter. But would he? Would he propose to a girl who was merely pretty but not beautiful? A girl with freckles on her nose, who had only recently been allowed to put her hair up? An orphan with only a bit of property in Northumberland and a vast knowledge of the romantic poets?

He had to. He just *had* to! Nicola felt it as surely as she felt that the colour ochre on a redheaded woman was an abomination.

Really, the only cloud in Nicola's otherwise sunny existence was Nathaniel Sheridan, who took every opportunity that arose – and there were many, as the two of them were often thrown together at various balls and assemblies – to tease and bedevil her about Lord Sebastian.

But Nicola tried resolutely to put Nathaniel from her thoughts as she penned her letter home, dwelling only upon the many merits of the God – to whom she correctly referred as Lord Sebastian in writing: only in her many private conversations with Eleanor, whom she saw with pleasing regularity, did she call him by their pet name for him – so that when she later wrote to inform Nana of their engagement – and please God, there would be an engagement – it would not be such a shock.

It was as she was describing the God's godlike dancing ability that Lord Sebastian himself walked into the room. Nicola hastily hid beneath a sheet of foolscap the lines she'd been penning.

'Good morning, Mother,' Sebastian said, stooping to kiss Lady Farelly, who sat writing her own letters in a robe of stunning blue satin that, to Nicola's knowing eye, must have cost at least as much as one of Lord Farelly's new hunters, of which he was not a little proud. 'I'm off to Tatt's to see a man about a horse. Is there anything I can get for you while I'm out?'

Lady Farelly made a distracted noise. She was busy writing letters of her own. Only hers were letters of regret, declining some of the many invitations Honoria had received to various balls and entertainments. A girl just out could be invited to as many as twenty events in a week, and had to be scrupulously careful which she chose to attend.

The wrong dinner party could result in a connection with a bad crowd from which a debutante might never recover.

His duty to his mother having been dispatched, the God turned his attention to his sister and Nicola. He did not have the teasing sort of relationship with Honoria that Nathaniel and Eleanor Sheridan shared. Instead, the viscount was unfailingly polite to his sister, which Nicola thought only right and proper behaviour, for a god.

'And how will you two occupy yourselves today?' he wanted to know, though the question seemed more directed at Nicola than at Honoria.

Still, it was Honoria who answered, as she flipped lazily through the pages of a copy of *Lady's Magazine*. Honoria disliked letter writing, and, being a bit of a standoffish type of girl, hadn't anyone to write to anyway, having made virtually no friends at Madame's other than Nicola – though Nicola knew the standoffishness was only to cover up a case of crippling shyness, stemming from Lady Honoria's insecurities over her somewhat horsey looks.

'We've got Stella Ashton's garden party,' Honoria said in a bored voice. 'Then supper and Almack's.'

'Of course,' the God replied. 'It's Wednesday; I'd quite forgotten.' He grinned at Nicola, who sat with what she hoped was a calm expression at the desk she'd appropriated, the one by the window with the view of the garden below. She trusted he couldn't tell how quickly her heart had begun drumming at the sight of him, so handsome in a spotless white cravat and a coat of hunter green. 'I suppose it would be too much to ask that we dodge Almack's this once. I've had quite enough of crowded assembly rooms, I think. What I'd like is a bit of fresh air for a change.'

Nicola, pleased to hear this, as she harboured no particular love for crowded dance halls either, said, ' "There is pleasure in the pathless woods; there is rapture on the lonely shore; there is society, where none intrudes, by the deep sea, and music in its roar."'

But the God, instead of uttering the last line, ' "*I love not Man the less, but Nature more,*"' said instead, looking impressed, 'I say, that's jolly good! Did you make that up just now?'

Feeling the slightest – only the slightest – pang of disappointment, Nicola said gently, 'No. It's Byron.'

'Oh, is it?' Lord Sebastian, looking supremely unconcerned, reached for an apple in a nearby fruit bowl, and bit noisily into it. 'Well, that's exactly how I feel. There was such a crush at Almack's last week. Can't we just skip it?'

Lady Farelly looked up at that, horrified. 'After what we went through to get tickets? We most certainly won't *skip it.*' Then she went back to her letters.

The God sighed, then sent a wink in Nicola's direction. 'Oh, well,' he said. 'I suppose I'll live through it, if you'll do me the favour of promising me the first and last dances, Miss Sparks.'

Nicola felt herself blushing. All of her disappointment with Lord Sebastian's lack of familiarity with the Romantic poets evaporated in her pleasure over his request.

'If you wish,' was all she said, however, and that she uttered with a demureness that would have well pleased Madame Vieuxvincent.

Grinning, Lord Sebastian left for Tattersalls, the horse auctioneers, and Nicola, smiling happily, returned to her letter. Where was she? Oh, yes. Describing the God. How could she do justice to those fine eyes and easy smile? It was going to be difficult, to say the least. She doubted even Lord Byron could do it properly.

Interestingly, it was as Nicola was carefully extolling all of the God's virtues in her letter to her loved ones back at Beckwell Abbey that Lord Farelly's butler entered the morning room to announce that two other personages for whom Nicola had pet names had come calling, and were waiting to see her in the drawing room – her cousin Lord Renshaw (the Grouser) and his son Harold (the Milksop).

Nicola made a face and laid down her pen. Lord Renshaw and his heir were just about the last people she wanted to see. Still, she supposed she had no choice but to spare a moment or two for her only living relatives, distant cousins though they might be.

Accordingly, she smoothed her gown and patted her upswept hair before sailing into the drawing room, her shoulders thrown back and her head held high, just as Madame had instructed all of her pupils. A lady, after all, never slouched or looked anything less than pleased while receiving callers, no matter how much she might happen to detest them.

'Lord Renshaw,' Nicola said, holding out both hands toward the spindly, nattily garbed man standing beside one of Lord Farelly's splendid marble fireplaces. 'How good it is to see you.'

Norbert Blenkenship – now Lord Renshaw, thanks to Nicola's father, who had left his title to his only living male relative, but all of the property that came with that title to Nicola – had been blessed at birth by neither fortune nor nature. He'd made up for the former inadequacy by marrying, through some miracle of fate, an heiress who'd had the good sense, after realizing what she'd done, to die. Nicola had always ungenerously supposed that the poor woman had rolled over one morning, got a good look at her husband, and promptly expired. In any case, she had left the unprepossessing Norbert the whole of her fortune, with the exception of what had been settled upon their only off-spring, Harold.

The real mystery, of course, was why the poor woman had chosen Norbert Blenkenship at all. Lord Renshaw was markedly unattractive. He had never, in the sixteen years Nicola had known him, smiled. Not even once. His thin lips seemed permanently set in a frown of disapproval, and he tended to dress in the sombre colours of an undertaker, though his wife had died long ago, several years before Nicola had been born. That, and his nearly constant complaints about everything from his health to the state of the empire, were what had earned him from Nicola the pet name of the Grouser.

'Nicola,' the Grouser said seriously, giving her fingers the barest of squeezes before dropping them. 'I see you are looking well . . . except for some freckles along the nose. Shame about that. You should be more careful. The sun can permanently ruin a lady's complexion. Still, you should count yourself fortunate that you have not, as I have, succumbed to the ague that is sweeping through this wretched town.'

As if to emphasize his words, the Grouser reached into his waistcoat pocket, withdrew a large linen handkerchief, and blew his nose into it loudly and lengthily, causing Nicola to regret having touched his hands a moment before, as doubtlessly they'd spent plenty of time recently in the vicinity of his nostrils.

While Lord Renshaw was suffering his latest round of ague, Nicola turned her attention towards his son, Harold Blenkenship – or the Milksop, as Nicola preferred to call him, though never to his face, of course. Harold, a dandy of the first order, always took the time to turn himself out in the finest and most up-to-date fashions, however hideous they might look on him, though he seldom seemed to take the time to make similar improvements to his mind, which was of a taciturn, sullen bent. Today the Milksop was wearing a velvet waistcoat and matching breeches in a startling shade of chartreuse. He looked, to Nicola's way of thinking, perfectly dreadful. But he didn't seem to know it as he preened before a looking glass at the far end of the room.

'Good morning, Harold,' Nicola called to her cousin. 'How are you today?'

The Milksop turned casually from his inspection of himself, then halted as abruptly as if he had been struck as his gaze fell upon Nicola. It took Nicola a moment to realize what had startled him so. He was used to seeing her in braids. It was the first time the Milksop had seen her with her hair dressed as a proper lady's ought to be. He looked as if he might faint from the shock of it. Nicola would not have been surprised if he had. Once, on a visit to Beckwell Abbey, the Milksop had fainted at the sight of a two-headed calf that had been born, and lived briefly, at one of the nearby farms. Though Nicola had been only six at the time, she had found her cousin's behaviour low-spirited in the extreme, and had silently christened him the Milksop as he lay in the hay and muck of the barn floor, moaning, until Farmer McGreevey poured a bucket of trough water on his head and thus revived him.

'Ni-Nicola,' the Milksop stammered now, staring at her as if she, too, had grown a second head. 'I . . . I . . .'

Since it seemed unlikely she was going to get anything sensible out of Harold, Nicola turned toward her guardian and said politely, 'Not that I am anything but delighted to see you, Lord Renshaw, but I am due to leave for a garden party shortly.' This was a lie, as the garden party was not to start for several hours, but as Nicola supposed the Grouser had never been invited to a garden party in his life, she doubted he would know what time they usually began. 'To what do I owe the honour of this visit?'

Lord Renshaw had put away his handkerchief. He cleared his throat several times before saying, 'Oh, yes. Yes. Well, you see, Nicola, something rather wonderful has happened.'

'Really?' Nicola raised her eyebrows and looked from Lord Renshaw to his heir. She could not imagine what sort of event Lord Renshaw would consider wonderful, but considering how dreadfully boring he was, she supposed he was only going to tell her that there was a sale of merino wool at Grafton House. 'And what would that be, my lord?'

And then Lord Renshaw did something so out of his normal character that Nicola, in her shock, quite forgot to keep her shoulders thrown back and her head held high. That was because, for the first time in all the years she'd known him, the Grouser actually smiled.

'We've had an offer, my dear,' he said. The smile was not a very good one. It was almost like a puppet smile, as if someone unseen above Lord Renshaw's head were pulling invisible threads connected to the sides of his mouth, causing them to turn upward, instead of down. It was, in fact, a rather frightening smile. Nicola found that she wished the Grouser hadn't attempted it at all.

Still, she asked gamely, 'An offer, my lord? Whatever do you mean?'

'Well, for the abbey, of course.' The smile, to Nicola's horror, grew even broader. 'An offer to purchase Beckwell Abbey.'

Three

'Beckwell Abbey isn't for sale.'

That was how Nicola had replied to her guardian's extraordinary statement that he had had an offer on her home. *Beckwell Abbey isn't for sale.*

It was a simple statement, but a true one. Thinking back on it, as she danced with the God that evening at Almack's, Nicola couldn't imagine how she could have put it plainer. *Beckwell Abbey isn't for sale.* End of conversation.

Except of course it hadn't been. Because the Grouser had gone on and on, explaining that Nicola was mad not even to consider the offer. For the abbey was a rambling, somewhat dilapidated structure that looked its age, which was considerable, and had the misfortune of being located only ten miles from Killingworth, a town where coal had been discovered, and which now hosted a colliery – a coal-mine over which a grey haze could be seen to hang on days when the sky was otherwise clear. She would never get a better offer for the abbey, and this one, at twelve thousand pounds, was really very generous.

Still, its state of disrepair and unfortunate proximity to a coal-mine notwithstanding, Beckwell Abbey was home, and not just to Nicola, but to Nana and Puddy and a half dozen tenant farmers, as well.

'But the offer is for twelve thousand pounds, Nicola,' the Grouser had explained excitedly – or as excitedly as the Grouser was capable of saying anything, which wasn't very. 'Twelve thousand pounds!'

Twelve thousand pounds was, of course, a staggering sum of money, considering that Nicola had barely a hundred pounds a year upon which to live. She might, as the Grouser was quick to point out, live comfortably for the rest of her life on the interest alone of that twelve thousand pounds, if it was invested wisely.

Except that Lord Renshaw was missing the point: Beckwell Abbey was not for sale. Nor, Nicola added, as she repeated this, was any of the land upon which it sat. The tenant farmers depended on Nicola's renting them her land for their sheep. Where were the poor things to graze if they hadn't access to the abbey's fields?

'Sheep?' the Grouser had burst out when Nicola had put this question to him. 'Who cares about *sheep*? You foolish girl, we're talking about *twelve thousand pounds*.'

Nicola, who did not appreciate being called a foolish girl to her face, could not quite understand what her decision to sell or not to sell had to do with the Grouser. It wasn't as if he would be enjoying any of the profits, since the abbey was hers. In any case, she had politely – Madame had instructed her girls very sternly that politeness was essential in all conversations, particularly ones with unpleasant relations – informed the Grouser that she hadn't the slightest intention of selling, and that he might give this prospective buyer her sincerest regrets.

To say that the rage this simple statement threw the Grouser into was extreme was as much an understatement as to say that the crowd here at Almack's tonight was packed in as tightly as fish in a barrel. Nicola had quite thought her

28

guardian would bite her head off. She listened to his ranting for a little while, then eventually stopped, and thought instead about Lord Sebastian, and his duck-egg-blue eyes. How much more pleasant to think of the God than of the Grouser!

'You seem far away, Miss Sparks.'

The deep voice, drifting across the dance floor, roused Nicola from her thoughts. She looked up and found herself looking into the very same eyes she'd been trying so hard to picture that morning during her unpleasant interview. *Good heavens!* This morning, all she'd been able to think about while talking with the Grouser had been the God, and here she was, dancing with the God, and all she could think of was the Grouser! How perfectly morbid.

'I *am* sorry,' Nicola apologized, as they waited their turn to make their way down the line of dancers on either side of them. 'I was only thinking about my guardian. He told me this morning that someone wants to buy Beckwell Abbey.'

'Well, that's a good thing,' the God replied. He was gazing about the room, his earlier protests that he longed for some fresh air evidently forgotten, since he looked to be enjoying himself immensely, despite the closeness of the room. 'Isn't it?'

Nicola didn't shrug, because that, of course, wouldn't be ladylike. Instead she said, 'I can't see how.'

'Oh, well.' The God held out his arm, as it was their turn to promenade. 'If the offer wasn't good enough, by all means, you've got to turn it down. Like this fellow at Tatt's today. Tried to sell me a horse he claimed was all right, but even a blind man could tell it was swaybacked.'

Nicola tried telling him that it wasn't that the offer hadn't been good enough; it was the *principle* of the thing. But apparently the God was not capable of deep conversation while also concentrating on a quadrille, since he looked a bit baffled. It was only later, having spied Eleanor entering the assembly rooms with her family, that Nicola was able to share her concerns with someone who was able to offer a sympathetic ear and heart.

'Oh, Nicky, how odious,' Eleanor cried. 'The Milksop, too? What was he wearing?'

'Chartreuse velvet,' Nicola said, and had to wait patiently for her friend's laughter to die down before going on, 'I just don't understand it.'

'Oh,' Eleanor said. 'I know. Chartreuse never looks good on anyone.'

'No,' Nicola corrected her friend. 'Not about that. About the abbey. Why would anyone want Beckwell Abbey? It makes no sense.'

'Still, twelve thousand pounds.' Eleanor shook her head. 'It's an awful lot of money, Nicky.'

Nicola turned a stricken gaze upon her friend. '*Et tu, Brute?*' she asked. But Eleanor only looked confused.

'Oh, Eleanor,' Nicola cried. 'From *Julius Caesar*. Don't you remember? We studied it only last term!'

Eleanor shook her head. 'How can you talk about Roman emperors at a time like this? Twelve thousand pounds could keep you in new lace mittens for years and years, Nicky.'

It was at that moment that the God walked up with two cups of punch, one of which he gave to Nicola.

'Here you are, Miss Sparks,' he said. 'Beastly stuff, but it does the trick.'

Nicola, catching Eleanor's congratulatory look, merely smiled and sipped her punch. She supposed she oughtn't feel so wretched. After all, here she was, having punch with the handsomest man in the room.

Still, it was a little unsettling that no one – *no one* – understood how she felt. She was thinking to herself, *I suppose I am being childish. I mean, it's true that I need the money more than the sheep need the grass. And I could always use a portion of that twelve thousand pounds to set Nana and Puddy up comfortably somewhere else, after all,* when Eleanor inhaled sharply and dug her elbow into Nicola's ribs, causing her almost to spill the contents of her punch glass down the front of the God's godly white shirt.

'Look,' Eleanor said in a hiss, gazing across the room with a shocked expression on her face. 'He's here!'

Nicola, assuming *he* meant the Prince of Wales, since it couldn't possibly mean the God, as he was standing there beside them, lifted a hand to her hair to assure herself that her ribbons were still in place. It would not do, she knew, to meet the Prince of Wales with her hair ribbons hanging down. Oh, if only she'd been able to get her hands on some face powder! Those freckles would be the end of her.

But then she saw that it wasn't a prince at all elbowing his way toward them through the crowd.

'Stuff and bother,' she said irritably. Because the Milksop was bearing down upon them at full speed.

Unbidden, her mind flew back to earlier that day, when the Grouser, having taken his leave of Nicola – in a thick cloud of disapproval – stalked from the room, leaving her alone with his odious son.

The Milksop, seeming to have recovered the use of speech, which he'd lost at the sight of Nicola without her braids, had asked her unctuously, 'You'll be at Almack's tonight?'

'Of course,' she had replied, in some surprise. The Milksop had rarely, if ever, deigned to speak to her after that

31

incident in the cowshed. In fact, this was the first time in nine years Nicola could remember him having said anything to her other than hello and goodbye.

But her astonishment was only to increase a hundredfold when the Milksop went on to ask, with a smile she supposed he'd been told was charming, but which she thought perfectly suspect, 'Then will you save the first dance for your cousin?'

Nicola only barely managed to keep herself from asking curiously, 'Which cousin?' before realizing he meant *himself*. The Milksop! The Milksop, who had never looked at Nicola with anything but contempt and disapproval for what he'd called her hoydenish ways – Nicola having had, in her childhood, an extreme love of mud tossing and tree climbing – had actually asked her to save a dance for him! What kind of ague had consumed him that he could, even for a moment, consider dancing with Nicola, whom he'd never made a secret of despising, especially after her having witnessed that famous faint?

'Oh. Er. Um,' Nicola stammered, perfectly unable to think how to reply. She was not accustomed to odious young men asking for her hand in a dance hours and hours before the actual event.

Then, with a rush of relief, she remembered the God, and was thrilled to be able to reply, demurely as well as truthfully, 'Oh, I *am* sorry, Harold. But my first dance for tonight is already taken.'

Harold began to look a little unsure of himself. Clearly he had thought Nicola would leap at the chance to dance with a young man as well turned out and stylish as he was. What woman wouldn't?

But he rallied enough to ask, 'The last dance, then?'

Lord bless the viscount. He really *was* a god.

'Oh, bad luck, Harold,' Nicola said with a kind smile. 'That one's taken, as well.'

An expression grew across the Milksop's ferret-like face that Nicola didn't recognize. That was because it was the first time she'd ever seen that particular emotion on her cousin's face. It turned out to be determination.

She ought to have known what his next question would be, but still, when it actually came, she was surprised. For a fainter, the Milksop was terribly persistent.

'The Sir Roger, then?' Harold asked in a deceptively light tone.

She couldn't believe it. He'd foiled her! Because if she claimed to be engaged for the Sir Roger de Coverley – a rowdy country dance that was *de rigueur* at balls all over England, and even, Nicola supposed, the Continent – and then she ended up, as occasionally happened, without a partner for it, he would know that she'd lied. She had no choice but to say, 'That would be delightful, Harold.'

And now here he was, coming to claim her hand for the Sir Roger, the first strains of which she could hear the orchestra playing. And though he had changed out of the chartreuse velvet and into finely cut evening clothes, they were still of a shocking shade of aubergine that only brought out the paleness of the Milksop's . . . well, milky-white skin.

'Oh, you poor thing,' Nicola heard Eleanor breathe, and then Harold was upon them, exuding milksoppiness.

'Nicola,' he said, bowing too low before her, so that his face almost brushed the knees of his purple breeches. 'You look exceptionally lovely tonight.'

Nicola felt her cheeks begin to burn, and not from the closeness of the room, either.

'Good evening, Harold,' she said, wishing that this morning, just this once, she'd worn her braids down instead of up. She was convinced this would have made all the difference to Harold's new attitude towards her.

The God, much to her chagrin, was regarding the Milksop with faintly raised eyebrows and a disbelieving expression, as if he could not quite decide what to make of the young man in the purple suit. Nicola could not blame him. She had never been certain what to make of Harold herself.

'Shall we?' Harold asked, holding out a hand that was almost as pale and slender as her own.

A lady, Madame Vieuxvincent had instructed her pupils, always accepted the inevitable with graciousness. Closing her eyes because she did not think she could bear it any other way, Nicola raised her hand to lay it in the Milksop's . . .

. . . and felt her fingers grasped by what seemed far too warm and sure a grip to be Harold's.

Her eyelids fluttering open, Nicola found herself looking up into Nathaniel Sheridan's clear, hazel-eyed gaze.

'Nicky,' Eleanor's brother said in a chiding voice. 'I can't leave you alone for two minutes without your giving away my dances to someone else, can I?'

Nicola was entirely too taken aback to reply. Whatever was Nathaniel talking about, her giving away his dances? He hadn't asked her to save any dances for him.

The Milksop seemed as confused as Nicola felt.

'Miss Sparks promised *me* the Sir Roger this morning, sir,' he bleated indignantly up at Nathaniel, who stood a good head and a half taller than Harold.

'Well, Miss Sparks promised it to *me* last week,' Nathaniel said.

And without another word, he pulled Nicola out to the dance floor, where they joined a group of other couples.

It took Nicola a moment or two before she was able to collect herself enough to ask Nathaniel just what he supposed he'd been doing, cutting in on her cousin in such a manner. The hostesses at Almack's were far stricter than Madame Vieuxvincent had ever been, and would brook no sort of disagreeableness from their guests, especially difficulties over dances and dancing partners. Woe be it to a girl who agreed to a dance without the direct permission of one of the hostesses. And woe be it to a girl about whom a gentleman complained of having been cut. If the Milksop said anything to anyone, Nicola would be in no end of trouble.

'Don't get yourself all in a tizzy,' was all Nathaniel would say about it, however. 'It isn't as if you *wanted* to dance with him. Why, in that colour, he looks exactly like a grape.'

'Still,' Nicola said crossly. 'You hadn't any right to—'

'Living with the Bartholomews,' Nathaniel went on as if she hadn't spoken, 'certainly hasn't done much to sweeten your disposition.'

'I could get in trouble if—'

'I didn't hear you protesting overmuch,' Nathaniel pointed out, and Nicola was forced to admit that that much, at least, was true. Dancing with anyone – even a poetry-hater like Nathaniel Sheridan – was preferable to dancing with the Milksop.

'Besides, he won't tell anyone,' Nathaniel said confidently.

Nicola glanced over her shoulder at her cousin, who was fuming in the far corner of the room. 'How do you know? Don't tell me *Harold* was at your college at Oxford, too.'

Nathaniel grinned. Nicola was disturbed to note that when he grinned, Nathaniel was almost every bit as hand-some as the God. It was a most dissatisfying discovery, as she was determined to hate Eleanor's brother for his negative attitude toward Lord Byron . . . not to mention oarsmen.

'Not hardly,' Nathaniel said. 'Let's just say I know his type.'

Nicola reflected that the Milksop's type was readily apparent in the way he was behaving at that very moment. He had stomped over to a refreshment table and was cramming as many confections as he could grab into his mouth, while all the while glaring moodily in Nicola's direction. It was exactly the way he'd used to behave when they'd both been much younger, and Nicola had refused to play with him, due to his tendency to have a tantrum whenever she beat him at games. Only then it had been Nana's famous ginger cake he'd stuffed himself with endlessly.

'How did you happen to become trapped into agreeing to dance the Sir Roger with Harold Blenkenship in the first place?' Nathaniel wanted to know.

Forgetting that she was piqued with him for his disdain of poetry, Nicola found herself describing to Nathaniel – whenever the dance allowed them to get close enough for speech to be possible – that morning's interview with the Grouser.

'You aren't going to sell, are you?' Nathaniel asked, as they stood opposite one another in the dance formation.

In spite of all her antipathy toward him, Nicola thought she could have kissed Nathaniel Sheridan. He was the first person to react to the news the way she had.

Though of course she could not act on her impulse. For one thing, it would be hugely scandalous to be caught kissing anyone at Almack's. And for another, she was in love with Sebastian Bartholomew, who probably wouldn't like it if he saw her kissing someone else. Or so she hoped, anyway.

'Of course not,' she said indignantly. 'I would *never* sell. Even if it *is* twelve thousand pounds.'

'That's probably why your father left the property to you,' Nathaniel observed. 'He didn't want the land parcelled out, and knew your uncle probably wouldn't scruple to do so.'

'He isn't my uncle,' Nicola replied, out of force of habit.

But there was something to what Nathaniel said. It was highly unusual to leave only a title, with no land, to one's heir. Was that why Nicola's father had made out such a curious will? Because he didn't trust his cousin Norbert? Nicola couldn't say she blamed her father: she didn't trust Norbert Blenkenship either.

'The real question,' Nathaniel said, 'is why anyone would be willing to pay so much for what is, from what you describe, a fairly unspectacular piece of property.'

'That's true,' Nicola said. 'The abbey hasn't much to recommend it, really.' Then, with yet another spurt of irritation, she added, 'Really, but it's inhuman of the Grouser to expect me to sell. Beckwell Abbey is all I've got.'

Nathaniel, who had not received instruction at Madame Vieuxvincent's, and so felt no guilt over shrugging, did so. 'It's more than that, isn't it?' he asked lightly. 'It's home.'

He was right. Beckwell Abbey *was* home. Nicola had never known another. She had enjoyed staying at Madame Vieuxvincent's, and had always loved visiting the Sheridans. And certainly it was nice living with the Bartholomews. But Beckwell Abbey was, always and for ever, home to her.

With a burst of feeling, Nicola recited, ' "I travelled among unknown men, in lands beyond the sea; Nor England! did I know till then, what love I bore to thee!" '

Nathaniel looked pained.

'Would it be too much to ask,' he wondered, 'that we forego Wordsworth during the Sir Roger?'

Nicola, though she tossed her head haughtily at this, could not help thinking, with a pang, that while he might claim to despise them, Nathaniel, at least, knew his poets . . .

Which was more than she was beginning to think she could say for Lord Sebastian.

But then the Sir Roger ended, and the God came to claim her for the last dance. And at the sight of Lord Sebastian's beautiful blue eyes, Nicola forgot all such disloyal thoughts. It wasn't for nothing she'd christened him the God, after all.

Four

'Papa,' Lady Honoria Bartholomew cried, bouncing a little in her carriage seat – something that would have appalled Madame Vieuxvincent, who had been very strict about bouncing, declaring it decidedly unladylike. 'Where are we going? Just tell me.'

But Lord Farelly only smiled knowingly and said, 'But if I tell you, it won't be a surprise.'

Lady Honoria let out a little shriek of frustration – Madame Vieuxvincent had also had some strong opinions on ladies who shrieked at anything but the occasional mouse – and turned to Nicola, who sat on the carriage seat beside her.

'Isn't he the most tiresome old thing?' Honoria wanted to know. 'Aren't you *dying* to know where we are going?'

Nicola, twirling a white lace parasol – Madame had never said anything against twirling – that she was using as protection against the fierce midday sun, only smiled and said, 'Indeed.'

The truth, she was almost as excited as Honoria. Lord Farelly didn't spend a great deal of time at home during the day. Nicola, not knowing much about fathers, having no memory of hers, supposed the earl was at his club, which was where wealthy noblemen in London seemed to spend most of their leisure time – although Honoria had mentioned that her father kept an office on Bond Street, though she had not been exactly sure what he did there.

So it had been quite a little shock when his lordship had appeared just before luncheon and announced that he had a surprise for them all.

Still, Nicola was determined not to let her excitement show. At least, she would not shriek, let alone bounce, as the Bartholomews' open carriage made its way through the crowded streets of London towards a yet-unknown location. That was because the God was trotting along beside the phaeton – he'd wanted to use the opportunity to give his new mount's legs a stretch. Nicola was therefore doing her best to appear cool and collected . . . a difficulty, given the summer heat. Still, the parasol helped a little.

And she certainly knew that, in her second-best white muslin gown, along the hem of which she'd spent all week sewing blue silk forget-me-nots, she looked very well. She'd sewn ribbons matching the shade of the forget-me-nots on to her white straw bonnet. Though her ensemble cost a fraction of the amount Lady Honoria's did, Nicola knew it appeared every bit as stylish and neat. And, careful as she'd been to keep her face in the shade, even her freckles seemed finally beginning to fade.

'Why, I know where we're going now,' Honoria declared, looking about. 'Euston Square.'

Lady Farelly, who had come along for the ride most reluctantly, as she disliked missing luncheon, and besides, had a dressmaker's appointment later in the day, looked about without enthusiasm. To her, London began and ended with Mayfair, and anything outside of it was simply tiresome.

'I hope, Jarvis,' she said to her husband, 'that wherever we're going, there aren't going to be monkeys. You know how I feel about monkeys.'

Lord Farelly laughed heartily, and assured his wife she had nothing to fear.

And then the carriage pulled to a halt beside a large crowd all clustered around something in the square that Nicola couldn't see. But others seemed to know what it was, since Lord Sebastian, dismounting, gave a knowing laugh, and said, 'Good show, Father.'

Nicola wasn't able to see what the surprise was until – the God escorting her and his sister most obligingly, while Lord and Lady Farelly trailed behind – they had made their way through the crowd. It was then that Nicola was met by a most curious sight. A circular fence had been erected in the square and within a ring of track was laid. On the track sat a monstrosity of a machine, with a barrel body and a stack jutting up from its top. Attached to the back of it was a landau carriage, converted to be pulled by the machine, rather than the more customary horse. Nicola, recognizing it from pictures she had seen, gasped.

'Why,' she cried, 'it's a locomotive!'

'Indeed,' Lord Farelly replied, beaming. 'Aren't you surprised? Isn't this diverting, my dear?'

Lady Farelly looked as if she wished the surprise had been champagne and strawberries at the Vauxhall. But she managed a small smile and said, 'Excessively, my dear.' Lady Farelly made no secret of the fact that she found her husband's obsession with locomotives almost as odious as she found monkeys.

Nicola, however, was quite impressed. She had never seen a locomotive before. She understood that locomotives were used to haul coal in some colleries, but she had never actually seen one. Now here sat one before her, not one mile from the centre of London!

'It's called the *Catch Me Who Can*,' Lord Farelly informed them, as proudly as if he had built it himself. 'Man named Trevithick set it up. And look.' He pointed. 'He'll let you take a seat on it. One shilling per person per ride.'

Nicola gasped as she saw several people, giggling excitedly, take seats in the carriage. A minute later, the engine gave a snort, and then, billowing white smoke from its snout and making a hideous noise, it began to pull the carriage around the track. The passengers laughed and waved at those watching from the crowd. They were travelling quite fast, about the pace of a horse at a brisk trot, and as they circled, the pace grew ever quicker.

'Oh!' Nicola cried. 'May we ride it, Lady Farelly? May we?'

Lady Farelly looked shocked. 'Certainly not!' she cried. 'What an idea!'

Nicola, a bit miffed at this, pointed at the people on the train as they went by. 'But look, Lady Farelly. There are children there. It seems perfectly safe.'

Lady Farelly gave a delicate snort. 'Safe,' she said. 'But hardly respectable.'

'I highly doubt,' Honoria agreed with her mother, 'that Madame Vieuxvincent would approve, Nicola.'

While this was undoubtedly true, Nicola could not help but feel disappointed. The *Catch Me Who Can* looked such fun! She longed to ride it.

Feeling someone's gaze upon her, Nicola tore her own from the little locomotive, and saw the God looking down at her.

'Do you really want to ride it, Miss Sparks?' he asked, looking faintly amused.

'Oh, yes!' Nicola cried enthusiastically.

Lord Farelly was digging into his pocket. 'Fortunately,' he said, 'I happen to have a few spare shillings.'

Lady Farelly glanced sharply at her husband. 'Jarvis!' she cried. 'You can't be serious.'

But Lord Farelly, looking sweetly sheepish, only shrugged. 'In a few years we'll all be criss-crossing the country in them like it was nothing, Virginia,' he said. 'It's only a matter of time.'

'Not me,' Lady Farelly declared with a shudder.

Nicola looked up at Lady Farelly appealingly. 'Please, my lady,' she begged. 'Look, it's slowing down. If we go now, we can get a seat for the next go-round.'

Lady Farelly looked heavenward – a sure sign, Nicola knew already from the short time she'd been staying with the Bartholomews, that the woman was softening.

'Well, if you must, I suppose I can't stop you,' Lady Farelly said unhappily. Then, as the God took Nicola's hand, eager to get to the queue already forming for the *Catch Me Who Can*'s next trip, she added shrilly, 'But if the thing should go careering off into the crowd and kill you, don't come crying to me!'

Excitedly, Nicola hurried – not running, because, of course, a lady never ran, at least in public – to secure a place in the queue, the God striding calmly along beside her. In the golden sunlight, he looked handsomer than ever – so handsome, in fact, that Nicola was conscious, as she passed the crowd gathered around the tracks, of the envious glances she received from other girls her age . . . girls whose mothers wouldn't let them climb aboard the *Catch Me Who Can*, and who didn't have as dashing an escort.

Really, Nicola thought. *I am being blown about life like a thistle after all. I truly am the luckiest girl in the world!*

It was just as she was thinking this that a voice called her name, and Nicola turned to see Eleanor Sheridan, along with the rest of her family, joining the queue for the *Catch Me Who Can*.

'Nicky, what are you doing here?' Eleanor cried, looking pleasantly surprised to see her. 'Don't tell me *you're* going for a ride on that thing!'

'Indeed I am,' Nicola declared excitedly. 'Lady Farelly said I might.'

Lady Sheridan, standing behind her daughter, threw a shrewd glance in Lady Farelly's direction. 'Oh, she did, did she?' she asked.

But, probably since Lord Sebastian was standing there, Lady Sheridan said nothing else, save, 'I'm glad to see my own sons aren't the only ones who've completely lost their heads over this railway business.'

Nicola smiled at young Phillip, who stood in line behind her, next to Nathaniel.

'Aren't you frightened?' she asked the youngest Sheridan.

As she'd expected him to do, the boy scoffed.

'Frightened?' he echoed disparagingly. 'Of what? *That?*' He added this as the engine pulled up just before them and the previous passengers began to climb out, looking no worse the wear for their adventure. 'Not on your life!'

Everyone laughed – all except Nathaniel, who just stared steadily, with what Nicola considered quite unnecessary hostility, in Lord Sebastian's direction. Really, she thought, but it was too ridiculous, this antipathy Eleanor's brother had against the God, simply because he happened to like to row and was, by all accounts, quite good at it. The two young men had a good deal in common, both being eldest sons and graduates of Oxford. One would think they might be friends.

But Nicola soon forgot all about her concern that the brothers of her two friends become friends as well, when the man operating the *Catch Me Who Can* turned toward them and called, 'Ne-ext!'

Lord Sebastian, handing over the shillings his father had given them, helped Nicola into the landau. As she lowered herself into the seat, she asked Eleanor, who'd remained standing while both her brothers took their seats, 'Aren't you coming?'

But Eleanor, with a quick look at her mother, who frowned, shook her head.

'Not in this gown,' Eleanor said, fingering the pale silk of her skirt. 'It looks much too dirty a business for me.'

Nicola had time for only a nervous glance at her own gown, with its row of brand new forget-me-nots, before the man at the controls called out, 'Hold on!'

Still, in spite of the warning, when the *Catch Me Who Can* lurched forward, it jolted Nicola with such violence that her head went snapping back on her neck, and she would have lost her bonnet if she hadn't flung up both hands to stop it from falling off.

'Are you all right?' the God asked concernedly, placing a long arm about the back of Nicola's seat.

Nicola, startled by the feel of his arm around her shoulders, looked up, and was even more startled when she saw how close Lord Sebastian's face was. Why, she could see each of his individual eyelashes! They were a delightful golden brown.

Then the train lurched again, and this time Nicola's head went snapping forward. Her whole body, in fact, might have sailed from her seat if Lord Sebastian's strong arm hadn't kept a firm hold on her.

And then, before Nicola could say another word, they were off.

Her first thought was, *Eleanor is wrong*. Because Nicola's white muslin skirt stayed perfectly pristine. That, of course, was because the white plume from the funnel before her wasn't smoke at all, but steam. Mr Trevithick's machine used water, which was heated by a coal-fired boiler to produce the steam which propelled it. It was amazing that as simple a thing as steam could create such a powerful driving force. The speed with which the engine chugged along was quite thrilling.

The breeze on Nicola's face felt refreshingly cool. And it was pleasant to whizz past the people gathered around the tracks, to see their shocked and delighted faces flashing past. It was the fastest Nicola had ever gone – she could hear Phillip bellowing that they had to be going more than ten miles an hour. It was certainly the most exciting ride she'd ever had.

And that, in no small part, was due to the strong, warm arm curled around her shoulders. Why, Lord Sebastian was holding on to her as if she were something highly breakable, or precious, even! She could feel his heart beating against the back of her arm. It was the most delightful feeling in the world. Surely it meant – it couldn't mean anything else, could it? – that the God liked her – more than simply liked her. Loved her, even. It had to! It just had to!

All too quickly, the *Catch Me Who Can* ran out of steam and chugged to a halt. The passengers, with much laughter and praise for Mr Trevithick, tumbled out of the carriage. Some – like young Phillip Sheridan, who had enjoyed his ride immensely – immediately ran back to the queue, another shilling at the ready. Others, like Nicola and the God, stood and gushed about what a glorious experience it had been. Still others, Nicola could not help noticing, stood

46

and looked disapproving. That, at least, was what Nathaniel Sheridan was doing.

I suppose because he thinks it isn't proper for girls to ride on the Catch Me Who Can, Nicola thought bitterly. Well, she would show him. She would go for another ride, just like Phillip was doing . . .

Except that just as she was opening her reticule to search for a shilling, Honoria came rushing up, followed by her parents.

'Nicola!' she cried. 'How was it?'

Nicola replied, loudly enough so that she could be certain Nathaniel overheard, that it had been perfectly delightful, and that she intended to do it again.

Lord Farelly, upon hearing this, burst into loud guffaws.

'See?' he said to his wife. 'See, Virginia? I told you. We'll make a railway enthusiast out of you yet, Miss Sparks.'

Nicola, her eyes shining, said, 'Oh, I should think I'm one already, Lord Farelly. Tell me, do you really think they'll have engines like this all over England one day?'

'Absolutely.' Lord Farelly, who was a big man, flung one arm about Nicola's shoulders, and another about his daughter's, and brought them both in towards his green velvet waistcoat for an enormous bearlike hug. 'All over England, all over the Continent . . . maybe even all over the world. People who think of trains merely as useful tools for hauling coal or timber haven't really thought it out. The most precious of cargo can be transported safely and quickly by railroad.'

Nicola, who felt her bonnet was being rather scrunched in Lord Farelly's embrace, exchanged a comic glance with Lord Sebastian, who stood nearby, grinning at her. 'Precious cargo?' Nicola echoed. 'You mean diamonds?'

'Not at all.' As abruptly as he'd grasped them, Lord Farelly released the girls. 'People, my dear. People! That will be the railway's true calling. Transporting people to their loved ones who live far away.'

'Oh,' Nicola said, tucking a few curls that had slipped from beneath her bonnet back where they belonged. 'I see.'

'If you are quite finished, Jarvis,' Lady Farelly said in a bored voice, 'might we go home now? I quite long for my lamb cutlet, which you so cruelly forced me to abandon in order to accompany you on this little . . . jaunt.'

Lord Farelly declared that they could and would go home now. And, after bidding polite goodbyes to the Sheridans (Nicola stubbornly avoiding the knowing grin of Eleanor – who was all atwitter over the way the God had draped his arm about Nicola – and the equally knowing gaze of Nathaniel, who had also witnessed it, and from right up close), they were all turning to do exactly that when Honoria, gazing across the crowded square, cried, 'I say, Nicola, but isn't that your uncle?'

Nicola looked, and was somewhat astonished to see the Grouser as well as the Milksop staring in her direction. The Blenkenships were not, of course, standing anywhere close to the queue for the *Catch Me Who Can*, the Grouser being too old, and the Milksop entirely too low-spirited ever to set foot on any such thing. Still, they had clearly come to observe others riding in the contraption . . . and the Grouser, in particular, did not look too pleased to see that one of those riders had been one of his own relatives.

Stuff and bother! Could Nicola never do anything to please the wretched man?

'He isn't my uncle,' was all Nicola said, but she raised a hand to wave to them, as they were too far away to call to. Ladies, according to Madame, never called greetings to anyone from across crowded public squares. The Grouser did not return the wave, but the Milksop did, all too eagerly.

48

'My goodness, Nicola,' Honoria said, taking Nicola's arm as the two of them strolled back toward the Bartholomews' carriage, 'but Mr Blenkenship seems to be holding quite a torch for you.'

It took a moment or two for Nicola to realize what the Lady Honoria meant. When she did, she was so appalled she stumbled to a halt and stared at her friend in disbelief.

'*Harold?*' Nicola cried. 'Oh, my lady, you must be joking!'

'Not at all,' Honoria said, looking puzzled. 'I noticed it at Almack's the other night, as well. He looks at you like . . . well, the way Papa looks at the *Catch Me Who Can*. I think he must be in love with you.'

Nicola was glad breakfast had been so long ago, or she was certain it would have all come back up. The Milksop! In love with her! Impossible!

Nicola shook her head. 'You are mistaken. The Milk— I mean, Mr Blenkenship only looks at me because he is so disgusted with my lack of business sense. His father wants me to sell my childhood home, you know.'

But Honoria was adamant. 'It's hardly disgust I see in his face when he looks at you, Nicola,' she said. 'Quite the opposite, I should say. I would have a care with him. You know what Madame said.'

Nicola did, for Madame Vieuxvincent had been quite firm on the subject: there was nothing on this earth that could do more damage to a girl's reputation than a string of lovers scorned.

But *Harold*? In love with her? Surely Lady Honoria was imagining things.

Fondly, Nicola patted her friend's arm and said, 'I will have a care, my lady, because you ask it. But I assure you, my cousin feels nothing for me.'

Indeed, Nicola was quite certain the Milksop was devoid of any proper feeling. For what sort of creature could pass up a ride, as he had done, on the cunning little *Catch Me Who Can*?

Because the thought was so utterly ridiculous, Nicola put it from her head . . . particularly when, at the door to the Bartholomews' carriage, Lord Sebastian offered her his hand to help her up the steps. In that instant, Nicola was flooded with the memory of how his strong arm had felt about her shoulders.

And then she could not, for the life of her, think of anything else at all. Well, what girl could?

Five

The Lady Honoria Bartholomew had not, it was true, been blessed by nature – at least not in the manner that her brother had. She was distinctly horsey about the face, and unfortunately possessed her brother's broad, athletic frame.

This would, Nicola knew, have not been such a disadvantage – indeed, it might almost have been a boon, for statuesque women could wear the high-waisted gowns that were so fashionable that season very well indeed – had Her Ladyship not insisted upon adorning her gowns and bonnets with feather trimming. In Nicola's opinion, feathers, on a large woman, looked ridiculous. What the Lady Honoria needed were clean lines and classic trimmings, to draw attention away from her heavy shoulders and thick waist and toward her better features, which included her really lovely thick blonde hair and exquisitely azure eyes.

What Lady Honoria needed, then, was not feathers, but braid and the barest minimum of lace.

Convincing Her Ladyship of the truth of this, however, was proving difficult.

Nearly a month had passed since Nicola had come to stay with the Bartholomews, and it was now approaching the height of the season. But Honoria, unlike a good many other graduates of Madame Vieuxvincent's, had yet to receive a single marriage proposal. It was not unusual that a girl like Nicola, who possessed such a small yearly income, and was freckled besides, had been overlooked by a good many of London's most eligible bachelors. But Lady Honoria? Why, she had nearly five thousand pounds a year! Horse-faced or not, she ought to have had suitors banging down the door . . . as Eleanor, who lived just a few streets away, did.

But Eleanor, of course, was a beauty . . . on top of which, having been Nicola's particular friend for so many years, Eleanor had learned how to dress. Feathers on Eleanor, who was petite, would not have been at all inappropriate. But on the Lady Honoria . . . disastrous! Nicola knew some drastic measures were called for, and so one morning, not long after their trip to the *Catch Me Who Can*, Nicola stood before the open doors of the Lady Honoria's wardrobe, a grim expression on her face, and a pair of scissors in her hand.

'They're all going to have to go,' was her final, very firm assessment.

Lady Honoria, perched on a tasselled stool some feet away, let out a sad cry.

'Oh, Nicola! No! Surely not all.'

'All,' Nicola said firmly.

Even Charlotte, the Lady Honoria's maid, who was French and knew instinctively that what Nicola was saying was true, could not help letting out a sigh of dismay.

'*Alors*,' she said to Nicola's maid, Martine, who had brought the scissors. 'Many 'undred pounds zey pay for each of zese gowns. Zey are from Paris.'

'It is too bad,' Nicola said, overhearing this. 'It cannot be helped.'

And, holding her scissors aloft, she reached for the first of the feathered monstrosities in her friend's wardrobe, and began industriously to clip away the soft marabou. 'We'll replace this,' she said, as she hacked, 'with jet beading. Martine?'

Nicola's maid consulted a box filled with assorted trimming that her mistress had collected over the years, and without which she never ventured very far.

'*Oui*,' Martine said, holding up a strand of black beads. 'Jet beading ready.'

'Excellent.' Nicola tossed the denuded gown to Charlotte. 'Next.'

They had made their way through almost half the contents of Lady Honoria's wardrobe before a housemaid tapped at the door and announced, when she'd been bidden to enter, 'A Mr Harold Blenkenship to see you, Miss Sparks.'

'Stuff and bother!' Nicola cried. She'd forgotten that the Milksop had written to ask permission to take her driving that morning. Under ordinary circumstances, she'd have declined the invitation with an apology that she had a previous engagement.

Unfortunately, however, she had already turned down five such invitations from Harold. Another refusal might be taken as insulting. As it was, she had had to apologize repeatedly for the incident involving the Sir Roger.

For, much as she disliked the Milksop, Nicola did not want to hurt his feelings. Madame had always been clear on one thing: friends can be shed like gloves, but your family cannot. Best not to antagonize them, as they will be around for a while.

'I must go,' Nicola said, giving her upswept hair a pat. Since it was only the Milksop, of course, she was not particularly concerned with her appearance. Still, she accepted the bonnet Martine brought her, one that she'd only just the day before trimmed in green satin to match a newly dyed green jacket. 'Kindly refrain from touching anything while I am gone,' she went on, with a warning look in Honoria's direction. She suspected the girl might try to salvage one or two boas, and that, of course, would be deadly. Nothing looked worse on a horsey girl than feathers about the face. 'When I return, we will go through the rest of your closet.'

Lady Honoria said nothing, merely looked sadly at the gowns Martine and Charlotte were stripping of fronds.

It was, Nicola supposed as she tied her bonnet strings into a neat bow beneath her chin, a hard thing to learn that, much as one might like feathers, they were not necessarily one's friend. This was true of many things, of course, not just feathers. The sun, for instance. She had the freckles to show for that. And many a woman had met her downfall through chocolate.

Still, if Lady Honoria had a hope of marrying someone at all presentable, she was going to have to surrender the ostrich down. She looked simply ridiculous in it.

And really, she ought to be thankful, Nicola supposed, that that was all she'd have to do in order to secure a husband. Many a girl had had to sacrifice far worse. Such as high-heeled boots.

With a nod at Martine, who nodded conspiratorially back, Nicola turned and went downstairs to meet her cousin.

Lady Honoria, Nicola soon saw, was not the only person in need of a wardrobe consultation. The Milksop was in another of his foppish sensations, this one in the form of fawn-coloured velvet breeches and a matching waistcoat. Over this he wore a coat in a shocking shade of aubergine. Nicola was quite appalled by the sight the two of them would make in Hyde Park, as her neat green jacket would look quite odd beside all that purple.

'Nicola,' the Milksop said, his piggy eyes quite lighting up when he saw her. 'A vision, as usual.'

Nicola was not used to Harold calling her a vision. Nor was she used to him following her with his gaze, as, she was realizing with a sinking heart, Honoria had been quite right about him doing. Ever since he'd seen her with her hair up, it seemed to Nicola that the Milksop had been paying a marked bit more attention to her than usual. Which was all the more odd when one considered that her feelings for him had undergone no such significant change. She still despised him quite as much as ever. It was all terribly puzzling. Why couldn't, Nicola wondered, Harold go and fall in love with a girl who welcomed his attentions? Why did he have to bother *her*? Why did everything have to be so *complicated*?

'Harold,' Nicola said to him, coolly extending a hand. Surely he could not fancy she felt anything for him but sisterly tolerance with a greeting such as *that*.

Much to her mortification, however, the Milksop did not shake her hand. Instead he raised her fingers to his lips and laid upon them several light kisses – right in front of the Bartholomews' butler, who was politely pretending he did not notice, but who felt, Nicola was certain, quite as embarrassed over the gesture as she did.

'Harold!' Nicola wrenched her fingers from the Milksop's grasp, and hurried to draw on her gloves. 'Really. What's come over you?'

But the Milksop only laughed in what Nicola supposed he considered a debonair manner, and swept her out the door to his waiting phaeton, which, to Nicola's relief, she saw was a smart vehicle in yellow and black, with a fine pair of matched bays to pull it. So at least she needn't worry about any foolishness over broken wheels or thrown shoes causing them to arrive home at some scandalously late hour, and –

perish the thought – forcing them to wed merely to save Nicola's reputation.

Still, just to be on the safe side, she said, loudly enough for the Bartholomews' butler to overhear, 'I simply must be home no later than one o'clock, Harold. Lady Honoria and I are going to Grafton House this afternoon to look at buttons.'

It was a lie, of course, but the Milksop did not need to know that.

Still, it didn't appear to bother him in the least that Nicola was deigning to give him only an hour of her time. After helping her into the carriage seat, he sprang up beside her and took the reins.

'You had better hang on, Nicky,' he said to her, with a smile she supposed he thought looked wicked, but which merely looked self-congratulatory. 'These are some spirited animals, and sometimes it's all I can do to keep 'em from bolting.'

Nicola, annoyed by this, because she was quite certain it was perfectly untrue, unless of course the Milksop drove his horses with such a heavy hand that they had occasionally to rebel, snapped, 'Well, then you had better sell them at once and purchase a pair you're better capable of handling.'

This was apparently not the response the Milksop had been looking for, as he appeared quite disappointed. Nicola supposed, with some disgust, that he'd been hoping she'd cry, 'Oh, Harold! Protect me!' and fling her hands around his arm. As if it had been she, and not he, who'd been too scared to try the *Catch Me Who Can*!

Looking irritated, Harold chirruped to the horses. As Nicola had expected they would, the fine animals broke into a steady trot without any sudden lurches, being well-trained and intelligent creatures . . . far more intelligent, she was certain, than their owner.

'I was quite surprised to see you at Euston Square the other day,' the Milksop began as they entered the park. 'I did not know you were fond of trains.'

'Oh,' Nicola said airily, keeping a steady eye on the carriages about them, and hoping that no one she knew would see her with a man who'd willingly wear such an ugly colour. 'I'm not particularly. But Lord Farelly adores them. And really, I found the whole thing quite diverting. It was thrilling to go so quickly.' She darted a sly look in his direction. 'Didn't you think so?'

Harold, as she'd known he would, looked embarrassed. 'Well, I didn't actually ride the thing. Looked a bit dangerous to me.'

Nicola, recalling how Harold had run from her any time she'd happened to dig up a worm to show him during his occasional visits to Beckwell Abbey, was not at all surprised to hear that so fainthearted an individual would find Mr Trevithick's invention threatening.

'What a shame,' she said, secretly thinking it quite typical of him. 'It was terribly amusing.'

'I suppose,' the Milksop said. 'Still, it was hardly the sort of thing I'd ever expected to see you take part in, Nicola.'

'Me?' Genuinely surprised, she turned to look at him. 'Really?'

'Well, you must admit' – the Milksop kept his attention on the reins, though the horses seemed hardly to need any direction, having taken to the track quite as if they did so several times a day, which, Nicola was certain, they most likely did – 'it wasn't the sort of thing one would hope to see a lady of one's own acquaintance doing. I mean, cavorting aback a ridiculous contraption such as that.'

Stung, Nicola retorted, 'For your information, Lady Farelly approved of my riding on it. Lord Farelly paid my way, for that matter. He says that one day, people – ladies as well as gentlemen – will think nothing of hopping on to a train and going miles and miles away from home.'

'That may be,' the Milksop said, 'but I didn't notice Lady Farelly riding the *Catch Me Who Can*. Or her daughter, for that matter. You were the only lady aboard, if I recall.'

Really, but this was just too much! It was quite one thing for the Milksop to pester her into going for a ride with him. But then to spend that ride rebuking her for taking part in something she'd had her host and hostess's permission to do! It was too much. If Lady Honoria was correct, and Harold was in love with her, he certainly had a strange way of showing it.

'I've had enough of driving today, Harold,' Nicola said with barely veiled anger. 'I think you had better take me back to the Bartholomews'.'

The Milksop astounded her by looking genuinely shocked to hear this.

'Good Lord,' he said, casting her a sharp glance. 'You aren't offended by what I said, are you, Nicola?'

'I most certainly am.' How could he doubt it? Was he as dense as he was cowardly? 'You've no business telling me how I ought to behave, Harold. You're only a second cousin, several times removed, if I'm not mistaken. And though you might be my elder by several years, I'm quite certain I could still thrash you, like I did that day you tried to keep me from going swimming.'

Flushing deeply at hearing this brought up – for it was a dark day, Nicola was sure, in any young man's memory that he happened to have been trounced by a girl – Harold cried, 'You were only six years old!' He glared at her. 'You might have been drowned!'

'In a stream only three feet deep?' Nicola's disgust with him deepened. 'There's the turnoff for Park Lane, Harold. Kindly take it.'

Only the Milksop didn't take the turn. Instead he pulled the horses to a halt and turned in his seat to face Nicola.

'I believe I have every business telling you how to behave,' he informed her with what, for the Milksop, was a good deal of forcefulness.

Nicola blinked at him. 'Oh? Pray tell me what makes you think so. Because I'd be very interested to learn it.'

'Because,' Harold said with an air of self-satisfaction that was quite unmistakable, 'I happen to have every intention of marrying you.'

Six

Openmouthed with astonishment, Nicola could only stare at the Milksop. Had he – or was it her imagination? – just proposed to her?

'Oh, yes, Nicky,' Harold said much too loudly, so that the people in the carriages passing by theirs – for Harold had already caused a disruption in the flow of traffic around the park by stopping in the middle of the track – looked at them curiously. 'You heard me correctly. We're getting married. I've already asked Father, and he's all for it. He intends to post the banns at once.'

Nicola, thoroughly nonplussed, gripped the sides of the phaeton and said to herself, *Whatever you do, don't laugh. Don't laugh, Nicola.*

But it was too late. A bubble of throaty laughter came welling up from deep inside and burst from her before she could stop it.

As she'd expected, the Milksop didn't at all appreciate his proposal being laughed at. He said with a forbidding glare, 'I'm quite serious, Nicola. And I would be a little more circumspect in my reaction, if I were you. You aren't likely to receive many proposals, you know, a girl in your position.'

'Oh, Harold,' Nicola cried, reaching up to wipe tears of laughter from the corners of her eyes. 'I *am* sorry. But you can't mean it. You know we shouldn't suit one another at all.'

'I fail to see why not.' Noticing finally the annoyed stares he was getting from the drivers of other vehicles on the path, Harold released his team, and they began again to circle the park. 'We have a great deal in common, you and I.'

Nicola was tempted to ask just what, precisely, the Milksop thought they shared in common, but decided against it. She wasn't at all convinced she could keep herself from chortling through his answer.

'Harold, it would never do,' she settled for saying gently instead. For, much as she disliked him, she could not help feeling sorry for him. That he should love her enough to want to marry her . . . well, that she had never imagined. She was very sorry she'd laughed at him earlier.

'Why not?' Harold wanted to know. 'I'm . . . well, fond of you.'

And with that, Nicola stopped feeling sorry for Harold. *Fond* of her? He was *fond* of her? She hadn't the slightest interest in marrying him, but she couldn't help thinking that if she had been so inclined, he'd have killed any such feeling right there. As a suitor, poor Harold was woefully inadequate. Where were the protestations of undying love, the flowers, the compliments? Why, he had not said so much that he thought her pretty!

Good Lord. He really was *such* a milksop.

'And Nicola, if you're thinking of saying no, I suggest you think again. You are going to have to face facts,' the Milksop went on. 'With an income as small as yours, you really aren't likely to receive any better offers.'

Nicola thought fleetingly of the God, and the way he'd flung his arm around her that day on the *Catch Me Who Can*. She thought of the number of times he'd asked her to dance, and how very well he'd looked each time, how manly and neat in his well-cut coats of muted colours. She recalled how *he* wasn't afraid to swim. After all, he'd been on his college's rowing team. Boats tipped, did they not? Oarsmen, therefore, of necessity learned to swim.

'I have two thousand a year from my mother,' the Milksop informed her matter-of-factly. 'And one day, of course, I'll be a baron. I don't think a girl in your position can expect a better offer. It really would behove you, Nicky, to give my proposal serious consideration. There aren't many men, I assure you, who'd be willing to take on a girl who not only hasn't a penny to her name, but is as . . . well . . . *headstrong* as you. Most men don't like a woman who does things like . . . well, ride behind steam engines in a public square.'

The Milksop was making it more and more difficult for Nicola to feel sorry for him. Soon, in fact, she'd positively hate him.

'Not *all* men would dislike it,' she couldn't help pointing out with some venom. 'Lord Sebastian, for instance.'

No sooner were the words out of Nicola's mouth than she wished them unsaid. But there was, of course, no help for it. The Milksop heard, and was immediately struck by not so much what she'd said, but the way she'd said it, if the startled glance he threw her was any indication.

'Lord Sebastian?' he echoed. 'You mean the viscount?'

Nicola gave a brief nod – there was nothing, she supposed, that she could do about it now. She only prayed Harold would not figure out the worst of it . . . her true feelings for the God.

Suddenly it was Harold's turn to laugh. Really. He did so, heartily and much to the apparent shock of the horses, who had clearly never heard their owner make such a noise before, as they'd turned back their ears and were rolling their eyes around in confusion.

'Lord Sebastian!' the Milksop cried. 'Oh, Nicola! You can't seriously think for a moment that the viscount has the slightest interest in you. Not *honestly*.'

Now Nicola felt even angrier than she had over his remarks concerning her behaviour in Euston Square. A surge of rage went through her that was quite as strong as the one she'd experienced the time he tried to prevent her going swimming. Only this time, unfortunately, she could not box his ears, because they were in public, and she was, thanks to a decade of Madame Vieuxvincent's tireless teachings, a lady.

'For your information,' Nicola, perhaps unwisely, but nevertheless quite coldly, said, 'the viscount and I are close friends. *Very* close friends.'

'Yes,' the Milksop said, sounding less and less, each time he spoke, like the Milksop, and more and more like a stranger, someone she had never met before, let alone was related to. 'I saw how *close* you two have grown that day at Euston Square.'

Nicola, in spite of herself, blushed. She knew she ought not to have allowed the viscount to keep his arm around her the way she had. But he'd done it only out of a desire to protect her, that was all. Fighting her embarrassment, she said stubbornly, 'Then you see what I mean, don't you, Harold?'

'Nicola.' Harold looked down at her very seriously. He was not handsome. He was too weak-chinned, and his eyes too small, ever to be called that. But when he looked very serious, as he did just then, it was hard to recognize him as the same person who for so many years Nicola had disparaged. There seemed to be a streak of stubbornness in him that Nicola had never seen before, a streak that had nothing

63

to do with courage or even spirit, but was nevertheless as indomitable as either of those qualities.

'You had better get it through your head that Lord Sebastian Bartholomew is never going to ask a penniless little-miss-nobody like you to marry him,' Harold said with chilling certainty. 'No matter how many times she lets him put his arm around her.'

Nicola, outraged by this, stood up in the phaeton, not caring if she tumbled out and met her death beneath a thousand hooves on the dirt path below.

'That's it,' she declared. 'That is *it*. Stop this carriage at once.'

The Milksop, looking more like his usual pale, scared self, hauled on the reins.

'Nicola!' he cried. 'Are you mad? Sit down!'

But Nicola didn't sit down. Instead, the minute the phaeton came to a halt, she clambered down from it unaided. The hem of her gown caught on one of the wheel spokes and tore, and she didn't even care. She merely yanked it free, turned around, and dashed across the carriage path, barely saving herself from being crushed by a passing chaise-and-four.

'Nicola!' thundered the Milksop from his driving seat. 'Nicola, come back here!'

But Nicola didn't come back. She didn't care if she had to walk the whole of the way home. She would gladly have walked all the way to Newcastle if it meant she'd never again have to be in the company of Harold Blenkenship.

As it was only just past noon, Hyde Park was teeming with visitors. It was no easy task, walking along the edge of the carriage path without getting knocked down. But she could not venture into the trees on either side of the path, as she'd heard footpads haunted them. She didn't care to have her reticule torn from her, for all it contained only five shillings and a few hairpins.

Still, she was vastly relieved when, from behind her, she heard a voice calling her name. It was not a voice belonging to the Milksop, who could not leave his carriage to chase after her on foot . . . not if he wanted to find his phaeton where he'd left it, as the park was teeming not just with those with the urge to see and be seen, but some less savoury individuals as well – footpads after bigger game than ladies' reticules. No, this voice belonged to a lady.

Nicola turned and was delighted to see Eleanor, her brother Nathaniel, and another man looking down at her in some astonishment from a handsome open-air carriage with seats for four.

'Nicky!' Eleanor cried, prettier than ever in a bonnet decorated with silk rosebuds that Nicola had trimmed for her just the day before. 'Whatever are you doing, walking by yourself, and along this dusty path? And was that the Milksop we just passed?'

'It was indeed,' Nicola said with a haughty tilt of her chin. 'I was forced to abandon his carriage, as he insulted me quite dreadfully.'

'Insulted you?' Eleanor looked shocked, but the gentleman in the driver's seat beside her only grinned, perhaps observing that Nicola appeared to have suffered no physical harm from her ordeal.

'Then you had better get in with us,' he said, 'where it's safe. Hadn't she, Sheridan?'

Nathaniel, in the opposite seat, said only, 'Indeed.' But he leaned forward, opened the door, and alighted in order to help Nicola in.

'Thank you,' she said most gratefully, as she sank onto the padded seat. 'I hadn't the slightest idea what I was going to do. But I knew I couldn't stay in that phaeton with him a second longer.'

'It's dangerous,' the gentleman said, still grinning as Nathaniel took the seat beside Nicola's, 'for young ladies to go driving without an escort. Fortunately Miss Sheridan has her brother here to protect her. And now you, I suppose.'

Nicola, looking from the gentleman to Eleanor to her brother and then back again, realized that she had stumbled into an outing between Eleanor and one of her suitors. Lady Sheridan, who always did what was proper, had undoubtedly insisted upon Nathaniel going driving with his sister and her newest beau. Certainly Nathaniel wore an air of brotherly concern usually reserved for dances or other such gatherings.

'Miss Sparks,' he said to her with unaccustomed formality. 'May I present Sir Hugh Parker? Sir Hugh, my sister's particular friend, Miss Sparks.'

Sir Hugh released the reins and turned around to shake Nicola's hand. She noted with approval that, though blond and with a moustache – so dangerous, if one hadn't the God's excellent bone structure to carry it off – he seemed nice enough, being both affable and tall. More important, he dressed neatly, and without affectation. His jabot was spotlessly white, something Nicola always liked to see in a man.

She wondered how much he had a year, and if Eleanor especially liked him. She couldn't tell by Eleanor's behaviour, which wasn't at all what it usually was. Not a giggle escaped her. Eleanor was trying to act like the lady Madame had attempted to train her to be.

'What a good thing we happened along,' Eleanor said as Sir Hugh urged his team of greys forward, once Nicola and Nathaniel had settled into their seats. 'What, precisely, did

66

your cousin do to insult you, Nicky? He wasn't bothering you about selling the abbey again, was he?'

'Oh, no,' Nicola said. 'This time all he wanted was for me to marry him.'

Eleanor let out a polite scream of disbelief, and Sir Hugh chuckled some more, as if he found Nicola highly amusing. Only Nathaniel took the information calmly, shooting Nicola a penetrating look, and saying, 'I take it all the answer the poor fellow received was no.'

Nicola, starting to feel a bit ashamed over her earlier behaviour toward the Milksop, said defensively, 'He isn't a poor fellow at all, Nathaniel Sheridan, and don't go trying to garner sympathy for him. It wasn't only that he had the impertinence to ask when, clearly, he's the last man in the world anyone would want to marry. It was the *way* he asked.' She was not about to share with another living soul what the Milksop had said about the God – well, possibly she'd share it with Eleanor when they were alone again together, but certainly not now, in front of Nathaniel and Sir Hugh. Instead she said, 'Why, all he said was that he was *fond* of me.'

Sir Hugh laughed outright at that, while Eleanor quite rightly looked angry on her friend's behalf. Only Nathaniel, folding his arms across his chest and leaning deep into his corner of the carriage, regarded Nicola with would have to be called scepticism.

'Let me guess,' he said. 'You'd have preferred to have heard something more along the lines of ' "Would that I were a glove upon that hand, that I might touch that cheek"?'

Nicola threw him a narrow-eyed glance, aware he was making light of her predicament . . . and of her love for beautiful language. Still, she was not about to pick a fight with her rescuers, so her retort was mild compared with how she would have liked to reply.

'A little Shakespeare,' she said primly, 'never hurt anybody. But if you think that my cousin Harold could have proposed to me in any manner that might have induced me to accept him, you are deluded. Still . . . well, a *few* compliments might have helped.'

'I am very glad you said no, Nicky,' Eleanor said, the bright sunshine bringing the russet highlights out in the chestnut curls that slipped from her bonnet. 'I should quite hate to see you married to a man who was your inferior, both intellectually and morally.' As she said this last, Eleanor threw a glance at her brother, who was still slumped in the corner of the carriage. 'Wouldn't you, Nathaniel?'

He merely lifted a dark eyebrow and regarded his sister sardonically.

'Wouldn't you, Nat?' Eleanor said more loudly.

'Wouldn't I what?' Nathaniel wanted to know.

'Wouldn't you hate to see Nicky married to a man who was her intellectual and moral inferior?' Eleanor said in a hiss, still trying, Nicola could tell, to act ladylike in front of her suitor, but really longing, Nicola was sure, to kick her brother. Though what Nathaniel had done now to upset his younger sibling, Nicola could not imagine.

'I suppose so,' Nathaniel said finally, straightening up. For once his expression was serious – although the lock of hair that was forever falling into his eyes somewhat ruined the effect.

'See here, Nicky,' he began in as stern a voice as Nicola had ever heard him use. Nicola had time only to wonder what on earth Nathaniel Sheridan could have to say to her in such a tone, and why his sister had turned away from her brother and was staring straight ahead with such assiduous concentration, when a familiar voice called, from quite close by, 'I say! Miss Sparks! Is that you?'

Nicola looked around and saw, to her utter delight, the God pull up in his brand-new phaeton, an even lighter and fancier model than Harold's.

'I didn't know you were seeing the Sheridans today,' Lord Sebastian said to Nicola, after greetings had been exchanged all around – rather grudgingly on the part of Nathaniel Sheridan, Nicola thought. Why did he always have to be so purposely rude to Lord Sebastian? 'Honoria said something about you going out with Harold Blenkenship.'

'I started off with Harold,' Nicola explained, 'but that didn't go well, and these fine people kindly rescued me.'

'Ah,' the God said, looking more godlike than ever in the bright sunshine that streamed through the leafy canopy the trees made overhead. 'That's a good one. I never pictured you in the role of knight errant, Sheridan. Surprised to see you lift your head out of your books long enough to give it a go.'

Nathaniel replied easily, 'Surprised to see you can make your way about town without an oar stuck up either sleeve, Bartholomew.'

The God, to Nicola's great astonishment, began to turn red. Nicola suddenly became aware of a tension in the air between Lord Sebastian's carriage and the one she was in. She had no idea where it had come from, but was relieved when Sir Hugh said, in his joking way, 'Gentlemen, gentlemen. Hadn't we better move along? We're holding up traffic here . . . '

Lord Sebastian, noticing the carriages lined up impatiently behind his, said, 'Damn my eyes if he isn't right. Come, Miss Sparks, I know you'll be eager to be getting home, and I'm going there now.'

Nicola, brightening, said, 'Oh, thank you, my lord,' and rose to leave Sir Hugh's carriage and enter Lord Sebastian's.

Except that Nathaniel, sitting by the door, didn't move.

'You needn't go,' he said. 'We'll take you home, Nicky.'

'Oh, thank you,' Nicola said, still standing. 'But it's out of your way.'

'Sir Hugh doesn't mind,' Nathaniel said. 'Do you, Sir Hugh?'

'If you say so, Sheridan,' came Sir Hugh's ready reply.

'Really,' Nicola said, beginning to feel a bit conspicuous, as the people in the carriages behind theirs were beginning to shout things like 'Get a move on!' and 'Horse thrown a shoe up there?' 'It's too kind of you. But Lord Sebastian is going right home. And I am expected soon, you know. Lady Honoria and I are . . . are going to Grafton House to look at buttons.'

It was a lie, of course. And not even a very original one. It was the same one she'd used with Harold. But for some reason, this time she felt guilty as she said it. Guilty? Why on earth should she feel guilty about lying to Nathaniel Sheridan? Why, he was never anything but unpleasant to her!

The lie, much as it bothered her, seemed to do the trick, however. There really wasn't any other way for Nathaniel to respond to it except by moving, albeit reluctantly, to help Nicola down from Sir Hugh's carriage, and then into Lord Sebastian's phaeton. Settled snugly into the seat beside the God, Nicola forgot her guilt as she excitedly waved goodbye to her friends. All but Nathaniel, who was in one of his sulks, waved merrily back. And then Lord Sebastian turned the phaeton around, and they left the park for home.

With what changed feelings did Nicola jounce along Park Lane coming home from the park than when she'd been going toward it! Then she'd been in thoroughly dejected spirits, thanks to her unwelcome company. Now she was sitting beside . . . well, a god. She was the envy, she knew, of every girl they passed. All of them were looking up at her, Nicola Sparks, and wondering how she'd come to have the great luck of capturing the arm of the best-looking bachelor in all of England. Well, the answer was easy enough. She'd let herself be blown about by life, like a thistle in the wind, and look what had happened!

'And what,' the God wanted to know as they made their way toward his home, 'did poor Mr Blenkenship do to you that you felt compelled to abandon him so cruelly?'

'Oh,' Nicola said distractedly, as she watched the sky passing above his golden head . . . a sky that came nowhere near the blue of his eyes. 'Asked me to marry him, is all.'

The God seemed to find this highly amusing. He laughed and said, 'A terrible crime indeed. And are you that harsh to all the supplicants for your hand, Miss Sparks? Or was Mr Blenkenship special somehow?'

'Especially offensive, maybe,' Nicola replied, adoring the way the God's eyelashes seemed to sparkle in the sunlight.

'Well, that's a relief, anyway,' the God said.

'What is?' Nicola asked, dreamily imagining herself touching those eyelashes.

'Well, that you aren't opposed to marriage in general,' the God said. And suddenly, with the hand that was not holding the reins, he reached for Nicola's fingers and brought them up towards his mouth. 'That means there's hope for me, doesn't it?'

For a moment, Nicola could only stare at him, hardly daring to believe what her own ears – and eyes, and fingertips, which were thrilling, inside her gloves, to the touch of his lips – were telling her.

And then, simply and directly, he dispelled any doubts she might have had.

'Marry me, Nicola?' he asked.

And even though Madame Vieuxvincent would have disapproved heartily, Nicola threw both her arms around the God's neck and kissed him, right there on Park Lane, in front of everyone.

Seven

And as simply as that, Miss Nicola Sparks became engaged to Lord Sebastian Bartholomew, the Viscount Farnsworth.

She was, to be sure, young to marry at sixteen. Yet, as Nicola was quick to point out, Juliet had been even younger when she'd married her Romeo. And Nathaniel Sheridan muttering, as he did upon hearing this, 'Yes, and look how well *that* turned out,' did not dissuade her. Nor did Lady Sheridan's assertion that she preferred a long engagement, and that, had Nicola been her daughter, she'd have made her wait two years, since she did not believe in girls marrying before their eighteenth birthday.

This only served to make Nicola grateful that it was Lady Farelly, and not Lady Sheridan, who was to be her mother-in-law. Two years! It seemed aeons to Nicola. She was miffed enough over the fact that she was going to have to wait a month before becoming Viscountess Farnsworth, as Lady Farelly needed that long to make all the arrangements and get out the invitations. Imagine having to wait two whole years!

And yet it was difficult for Nicola to be unhappy about much of anything . . . not now that she had, at long last, her heart's desire. For what girl wouldn't wait a month, or even two, for the privilege of marrying a young man like the

God? Nicola could not think of one. She was the envy of her entire set. Even Honoria was jealous . . . though not, of course, for the same reason Stella Ashton, another graduate of Madame Vieuxvincent's, was. No, Honoria was envious because Nicola had had two – two! – proposals in one day, while Honoria still hadn't had even one.

'Just wait,' Nicola had told her. 'Wait until Charlotte and Martine finish removing all the feathers. You'll have proposals galore.'

Though it was hard for Nicola to think about anyone, really, other than herself, in her current state of joy. Especially when everyone – everyone besides the Honorable Nathaniel Sheridan, that is – was so full of congratulation and joy over Nicola's engagement. Nana wrote from Beckwell Abbey, offering Nicola her best wishes, and promising to prepare for the bride and groom her famous ginger cake upon their first visit to Northumberland as a married couple. Madame Vieuxvincent sent a congratulatory note, along with a copy of Mary Wollstonecraft's *A Vindication of the Rights of Woman*, a must-have, she wrote, for every bride preparing to begin a family.

Even the Milksop, being the milksop that he was, sent Nicola a nosegay, along with his sincerest – or so he wrote, anyway – wishes for a happy marriage. That, coupled with his father's grudging agreement to loan Nicola enough money to outfit herself with a smart trousseau, made her happiness quite complete. The Grouser even went so far as to give Nicola his blessing . . . though grudgingly.

'I suppose,' he'd said, coming to call upon Nicola shortly after the news reached him, 'you know your own mind. Though I must say I think my Harold's twice the man your viscount is.'

Nicola kept her own opinion on this matter to herself.

But her delight – over the man she loved proposing, her love for her future in-laws, the fact that she was soon to be a viscountess – was not as easy to keep inside.

And, more often than not, the place where it all came bursting out was in the company of Eleanor Sheridan. Nicola couldn't really enthuse about her good fortune in front of her fiancé's sister – not when Honoria hadn't a beau, or even a hope of one, of her own. But Eleanor had had some exciting news as well: Sir Hugh had, like the God, proposed, and been accepted. The couple would have to wait two years before the nuptials could take place – how Nicola pitied her friend! – but were otherwise ecstatically happy. As Sir Hugh had five thousand a year and a manor house in Devonshire – not to mention a seemingly endless supply of clean white cravats – Nicola approved of this match for her friend, in spite of the moustache.

But her surprise that her friend did not quite return the feeling where Nicola and the viscount were concerned was considerable.

'It's only,' Eleanor explained, when Nicola demanded to know just what she meant when Eleanor made the astonishing admission that she wasn't certain the God was quite as godlike as they'd once thought, 'that Nat told me some things . . . '

'Oh, Nat,' Nicola scoffed as she stooped to examine a bonnet she admired in the window of a milliner's shop on fashionable Bond Street. 'Don't tell me you're listening to anything your brother says. He has an unfair – and, I'm sure, entirely unfounded – prejudice against Lord Sebastian.'

'It isn't only prejudice, Nicky,' Eleanor said gravely. Since meeting Sir Hugh, Eleanor had become markedly less silly.

She was, at times, even serious. It was as if Sir Hugh's lighthearted good humour was enough for both of them, and so Eleanor had been forced to take over the role of the staid adult in their relationship. ''Nat heard some very bad things about your Lord Sebastian, back when he was at Oxford.'

'My Lord Sebastian!' Nicola cried, straightening up. 'Oh, I like that! Not two months ago, he was the God to you, and now he's "my Lord Sebastian".'

'Nicky,' Eleanor said. 'Do be serious. Do you know Lord Sebastian gambles? And not just at cards and bagatelle, either, but on horses.'

'So does the Prince of Wales,' said Nicola, who had known this, and was a bit troubled by it, but supposed it was simply one of those things men did, and that there was no help for it.

'But that isn't all, Nicky. You know he never so much as opened a book the whole of the time he was at college? He only passed because Balliol hadn't had a winning rowing team in years, and the deans didn't want to send down their best oarsman.'

'Stuff and bother,' Nicola said, twirling her parasol in an agitated manner. 'That's nothing but unsubstantiated rumour. Really, Eleanor, I would think you would know better than to go telling tales . . . '

'Nicky,' Eleanor said, quite as seriously as she'd ever spoken. 'I know he's handsome. And I know he's rich. But how is he as a person? Do you even know?'

'For heaven's sake, Eleanor,' Nicola said. 'Of course I do. He's the kind of person who wants to marry me. Isn't that enough?'

Before Eleanor had a chance to answer this question, however, the topic of their conversation himself suddenly turned up, looking dapper in a new top hat and morning coat, and jauntily swinging a silver-tipped cane.

'Good heavens,' he cried upon recognizing Nicola and Eleanor, to whom he'd tipped his hat out of force of habit while strolling past them. 'What a stroke of luck! I only stepped from my club for a moment for a bit of air, and what do I find just outside the door? Two of the loveliest ladies in London. Which direction are you going? I'll walk with you.'

Eleanor, turning a delicate shade of crimson over having so very nearly been caught speaking ill of the viscount by the man himself, sputtered, 'Oh, no need, no need, my lord. We are waiting here for my brother and Sir Hugh. They've gone into the tobacconist's, and should be back in a moment.'

'My good fortune, then,' Lord Sebastian said gallantly. 'I shall wait with you until their arrival. Now, what are we discussing? The weather, which is lovely? Or yourselves, which is even lovelier?'

Nicola giggled at her betrothed's wittiness (though she could not help silently questioning his grammar). Eleanor, however, did not look at all impressed. In fact, she seemed flustered, and kept glancing over her shoulder, as if eager for her brother and Sir Hugh to reappear. It dismayed Nicola no end that the two people who were most important to her in the world could not be better friends. And so while they stood there, she attempted to calm Eleanor's fears for her future happiness by proving them completely unfounded.

'It's such a coincidence that you happened upon us just now, my lord,' she said, with all the kittenish charm she could muster, 'as Eleanor was just quizzing me about you.'

77

'Me?' The God had taken his gold watch from his pocket and was examining it. 'What about me?'

'Yes, exactly,' Nicola said with a laugh, slipping her hand through the crook of his arm. 'Eleanor wants to know all about you.'

The God blinked his lovely blue eyes. 'Oh, I see. Well, not much to know, is there? What you see is what you get.'

'That's what I was telling her,' Nicola said, giving his arm a happy squeeze. 'You are like an open book.'

'Indeed,' the God agreed. 'Though a bit of a dull one, I'm sorry to say. Some dusty old thing by Walter Scott, I should think.'

Nicola, wincing a bit at hearing her favourite author called dull, nevertheless pressed on in her campaign to win Eleanor's approval of her beau.

'Precisely,' she said, with what she hoped was a winning smile. 'Now, why don't you tell Eleanor that diverting story you were telling me last night.' When Lord Sebastian looked blank, Nicola prompted him, 'You remember, about the gelding you wished to purchase at Tattersall's the other day.'

'Oh,' the God said, brightening. 'That story. Course. Demmed amusing, that was. There was this gelding, see—'

But the God's amusing story about the gelding was interrupted when a grubby little hand reached up to tug upon his sleeve.

'Pardon, sir,' a childish voice lisped. 'But ken you spare a penny for a poor orphan?'

Lord Sebastian jerked his arm away from the tiny, much begrimed fingers that had deigned to touch it and cried, instinctively raising the silver-tipped cane, 'See here! What do you think you're doing?'

The child – for, though it was so thoroughly covered in

dirt and ash that its gender was nearly impossible to distinguish (though Nicola suspected by the length of the creature's hair that it might be female) its lack of stature indicated someone not yet fully grown – cowered, throwing up an arm to protect herself from the blow she clearly expected to be forthcoming.

'Oh, please, sir,' the child cried. 'I din't mean to dirty it! I'm sorry, sir! I'm sorry!'

Nicola – not because she actually thought the viscount might strike the little girl, but because it seemed the sensible thing to do – moved quickly to step between the God and the street urchin.

'Of course you didn't mean to soil the gentleman's coat,' she said, more calmly than she felt. 'You only startled Lord Sebastian. Didn't she, my lord?'

The God lowered the cane, looking extremely vexed. His gaze was on his sleeve.

'This is a brand-new coat,' he declared in an indignant tone. 'And look here, Nicola, there're fingermarks on it.'

'She didn't do it on purpose,' Nicola said. 'Did you, dear?'

But the little beggar child was crying too hard to reply, having been frightened by the cane the gentleman had waved so threateningly above her head.

'There, there,' Nicola said, opening her reticule and leaning down to apply a clean white handkerchief to the child's tears. 'None of that. Lord Sebastian is sorry he startled you.'

'Sorry?' The God was industriously applying a handkerchief of his own to his cuff. 'I should say not. Look at this dirt, Nicola. It isn't going to come out. The coat's ruined.'

'A little soda water when we get home,' Nicola said to the God, 'will take care of it.' To the beggar child, Nicola said,

'Here, take this.' Then, putting her handkerchief away, she slipped the little girl a shilling from her bag. A shilling was, of course, a small fortune . . . enough for a ride on the *Catch Me Who Can*, and more than enough for a meat pie. The little girl's weeping stopped the moment she laid eyes upon the coin.

'Good Lord, Nicola,' the God said with some disgust as the child, her tears evaporating as quickly as they'd appeared, seized the money and ran off with a glad cry of thanks. 'You actually gave that creature a shilling after the way she pawed me? What can you be thinking?'

Nicola closed the drawstrings of her bag. 'Well, of course I did,' she said with some asperity. 'Didn't you see her? She was half-starved, poor little thing.'

'Well, you'd be half-starved, too,' Lord Sebastian declared, irritated, 'if every penny you scraped went to buy drink for your mother.'

'She said she's an orphan,' Nicola reminded him with some feeling. 'She doesn't have a mother.'

'Of course she does, Nicola.' The God sighed with a roll of his beautiful eyes. 'They all say they're orphans. But believe me, that child's got a mother somewhere, and a father, too, I shouldn't wonder. And the whole family's making a healthy living off tenderhearted souls like you. Who, I might add, don't have a good deal of money to be wasting on worthless refuse like that.'

Nettled, Nicola said, 'You don't know she wasn't telling the truth, my lord.' Nicola felt, for reasons she could not explain, extremely vexed with him, and so spoke more sharply than perhaps the situation warranted. 'You don't know anything about it at all.'

It was excessively unfortunate that at this precise moment, Nathaniel Sheridan and Sir Hugh suddenly appeared.

'What doesn't Lord Sebastian know?' Sir Hugh demanded in his usual lighthearted manner.

'Anything at all, apparently,' the God replied, with equal jocularity.

Sir Hugh looked from Nicola's face – which she was certain was hot with embarrassment and not a little anger – to Lord Sebastian's, which was, as always, coolly handsome, and gave a low whistle.

'We arrived just in time, I see,' he said, nudging Nathaniel with his elbow, 'to witness the happy couple's first lovers' quarrel.'

'It isn't a quarrel,' Eleanor spoke up, to Nicola's immense relief. 'Nicola merely gave some money to an orphaned beggar child, and Lord Sebastian suggested she might do better to save her pennies for a worthier cause.'

'Ah,' Nathaniel said, with a knowing glance in Nicola's direction. How infuriating that he, of all people, should happen to show up now, of all times, just when she and Lord Sebastian were having an argument . . . not even an argument, either, but merely a . . . a . . . disagreement! And a very minor one, at that. It was too bad that Nicola could never seem to manage to maintain an air of cool detachment in front of Eleanor's brother, as Madame had always suggested a lady should.

'But there's the rub,' Nathaniel said, managing an air of cool detachment, Nicola couldn't help noticing, himself. 'Nicola, being an orphan, can hardly be expected to resist appeals for help from other orphans, especially those less fortunate than herself.'

This was so close to how Nicola felt about the situation that she very nearly cried out. How on earth could Nathaniel have known? It was almost as if he had read her mind.

'Oh, come now,' Lord Sebastian said dismissively. 'Nicola can't possibly think she has anything in common with those little pieces of trash that litter the streets, grubbing for coins. Do you, Nicola?'

Feeling the God's cool gaze on her, Nicola coloured, as she nearly always did whenever he looked in her direction. How could she help but blush, given that the God was quite the handsomest man in the world? And he was, miracle of miracles, hers. All hers.

But even gods sometimes made mistakes.

'Of course,' she replied, attempting to keep her tone as dismissive as his. 'An orphan is an orphan, after all. And it really is only by the grace of God that I never had to live the way that poor child lives. My father, at least, left me more or less well taken care of. So many orphans haven't the sort of luck I've had.'

This was, Nicola felt, quite an impressive speech. She saw admiration in Eleanor's warm glance. Even Sir Hugh looked impressed.

And Nathaniel? Well, Nathaniel Sheridan was never in the least admiring of anything Nicola ever did. But even he, just this once, looked less inclined to laugh at her than usual.

Unfortunately, however, the God did not seem to share Nathaniel's inclination, since he laughed quite heartily and, taking Nicola's hand, cried, 'Oh, but you are an enchanting creature, I swear! As if *you* could ever find yourself in a situation at all like that pitiful child's. Why, orphan though you may be, Nicola, you could never find yourself friendless and alone, begging for scraps to eat. You're entirely too pretty.'

And though this was, of course, a flattering thing to say, Nicola could not help thinking that the God had rather missed the point of her speech.

Still, she forgave him, because he seemed really to mean what he'd said. And what kind of girl could hold a grudge for long against a fellow as handsome as Lord Sebastian? Not Nicola, that was for certain.

Though she was careful after that to steer him well out of the path of any beggar children she happened to spy.

Eight

'He's the kind of person who wants to marry me,' Nicola had said to Eleanor about the viscount. 'Isn't that enough?'

But later, alone in her room at the Bartholomews', Nicola couldn't help wondering if it really was. After all, the Milksop had wanted to marry her, as well, and look what kind of person he was: the kind who fainted at the sight of the merest animal oddity, and who implied that a girl like Nicola could not possibly know how to swim, let alone be loved by a young man like the God. A nasty, horrid person. That was what Harold Blenkenship was.

Lord Sebastian wasn't nasty or horrid. Yes, he did seem a bit lacking in tolerance for beggar children. But then, who *liked* seeing beggar children? It was sad always to see them on the street, holding out their dirty little hands for coins that – the God was probably quite right – only went to buy drink for their slatternly parents. Nicola could not blame him for having an aversion to such creatures. And though Nicola had managed, with soda water, to get out the stain from Lord Sebastian's coat, it was true that it had taken quite a while, and the sleeve never did look quite as nice as it had before.

And yes, it was true the God had a temper. Nicola's first glimpse of it, the day he'd raised his cane as if to strike that poor child, had been a startling one. But most men had tempers. It wasn't necessarily a bad thing. And indeed, Lord Sebastian hadn't, in the end, struck the child. Clearly he had control of his temper. And that was more than could be said of many men.

And Nicola had never once seen the God strike any of his horses. Quite the opposite, in fact. His affection for the creatures was touching to behold.

And yes, certainly Lord Sebastian did seem to enjoy a game of whist. But that didn't make him an inveterate gambler. He merely loved the thrill, the exhilaration of the game!

And while he might be unfamiliar with the works of most of the poets Nicola admired, that certainly didn't make him a dunce. Lord Sebastian was just an athletic sort of person who hadn't time to read, between all of his shooting outings and games of bagatelle.

Nathaniel, who wasn't much of an athlete – oh, he rode, Nicola knew, but he wasn't fond of shooting, and he was even less fond of bagatelle – and who seemed to think that a good day was one spent adding up long columns of numbers on behalf of his father's estate manager, would naturally dislike a fellow like Lord Sebastian, if only because their natures were so very disparate. It was, as Nicola had said to Eleanor, entirely a matter of prejudice. Nathaniel was prejudiced against the God for the simple reason that the God was so unlike him. It would, she assured Eleanor, pass, as Nathaniel and the God got to know one another better.

But until it did, things were not going to be pleasant between Nicola and her best friend's brother. This became clear the very next night, when Nicola happened to run into Nathaniel Sheridan at – where else? – Almack's.

He was getting punch. Nicola, who'd already had her three dances with the God that evening, had not felt right accepting invitations from anyone else for the next set – after all, she was virtually a married woman – and had instead gone to find something to drink, as the room was hotter even than usual. She spied Nathaniel at the refreshment table. Otherwise, she would not have ventured near it. Her engagement was still so new, she felt protective of it. She did not want to hear it – or her future husband – maligned by anyone, even in a teasing manner.

She needn't have worried. Nathaniel saw her – she was quite sure he saw her. Their gazes met above the crystal punch bowl. And yet he did not say a word. He merely lifted the two glasses he held – apparently he'd been getting punch for someone else in addition to himself – and walked away, his well-tailored black evening coat melting into a sea of similar coats, until Nicola could not make him out anymore.

Stunned, Nicola stood where she was for a full minute before the enormity of what had just happened sank in fully: Nathaniel Sheridan had cut her!

Nicola had heard about cutting before, of course. Madame had warned them most seriously about the dangers of cutting – or socially ignoring another person with whom one was very much acquainted. Cutting was ill-mannered, immature and just about the cruellest thing one person could do to another.

Even so, sometimes cutting was necessary. Overzealous suitors sometimes had to be cut in order for a lady to preserve her reputation. And of course if one girl was spreading slanderous rumours about another, the girl about whom the rumours were focused had every right to cut her slanderess.

But for Nathaniel Sheridan to cut her, Nicola Sparks, his sister's most particular friend? There was no excuse for such behaviour!

Well, if he thought he was going to get away with it, he had another think coming entirely. Nicola was not the type of girl to meekly accept such a slight.

Accordingly, setting down her punch glass, Nicola flung herself into the sea of black coats into which Nathaniel had just disappeared, determined to find him, and then make him apologize for his unspeakably rude behaviour. This was not the course of action Madame Vieuxvincent recommended to her pupils who found themselves in the ignominious position of being cut. Confronting the cutter was not the prescribed method for solving the problem. But Nicola was too angry to think what Madame would have wanted her to do. All she could think was that Nathaniel Sheridan was going to rue the day he'd ever cut Nicola Sparks.

Which might have been why, when the God came up to her a second later, she brushed him off with a curt, 'Not now, my lord.' She had no time for gods just then. She had a mortal she needed to set straight about a few things.

She found him standing by a window, chatting amiably with Miss Stella Ashton, who wore a dress in a hideous shade of yellow that made her skin look far more sallow than it actually was. It was for Miss Ashton that he'd brought the punch glass. They were both looking down at something on the street below, and laughing.

Laughing! Nicola felt as if she might burst into flames on the spot, she was so angry.

'I beg your pardon,' she said, intruding upon a private conversation (Madame would most certainly not have approved).

Stella Ashton looked up from her punch glass and said sweetly, 'Oh, Miss Sparks. Good evening.'

'Good evening, Miss Ashton,' Nicola said with a nod. To Nathaniel, who was looking at her as if she were a madwoman, she said, 'May I have a word with you, Mr Sheridan? *Alone?*'

Nathaniel lifted one of his dark eyebrows in obvious amusement. But all he said was, 'Certainly.' He set his punch glass down upon the window sill, and bowed to the sallow-faced Stella. 'Would you excuse me for a moment please, Miss Ashton?'

Stella blinked her big – and, in Nicola's opinion, vapid – eyes and said, 'Why, of course,' in a confused manner, as if Nicola, instead of asking permission to steal away her escort for a moment, had announced that the room were on fire.

A moment later, standing some feet away in a darkened corner of the room, out of the range of the dancers and at some distance from the musicians, so the noise was not quite as oppressive, Nicola whirled to face Nathaniel. She was a bit alarmed to find, when she did so, that Nathaniel's face was only a few inches from hers. She had not been aware he'd been standing quite so close to her. Still, backing down would look as if she were intimidated by him, which she most certainly was not.

'Just who,' she demanded in a voice just loud enough to be heard above the music, but not loud enough for Stella Ashton, who was looking at them very intently indeed, to overhear, 'do you think you are, Nathaniel Sheridan, to cut me?'

He had the decency to blush, at least. Looking abashed, that familiar lock of hair falling over his eyes so that she could not read them, he said, 'I didn't cut you, Nicky. I mean, Miss Sparks.'

'You most certainly did,' Nicola declared. 'You looked right at me at the punch bowl just now, and then turned around and walked away without saying a word!'

'Because I couldn't,' Nathaniel said, 'think of anything to say.'

'Oh, and I suppose "Good evening, Miss Sparks" would have been too banal for someone of your great mental prowess?' She felt quite proud of herself over that one. Nathaniel Sheridan *was* too impressed with himself by half. Imagine thinking poetry a waste of time!

'I ought to have said good evening,' came Nathaniel's unexpected reply. 'You're quite right.'

Nicola, having anticipated a battle of much longer and more heated duration, was taken aback by this sudden capitulation. She had never known Nathaniel to agree so readily to an accusation she'd put to him.

'Are you quite well?' she asked a bit worriedly.

Nathaniel regarded her steadily, his eyes still shadowed so that she could not read them. 'Of course I am,' he replied. 'Why do you ask?'

'Well, because it isn't like you to actually let me win an argument.' Nicola studied him through narrowed eyes. 'Are you sure you aren't suffering from an ague?'

'Yes,' Nathaniel said, and he suddenly tossed his head so that the lock of dark hair was flung back, and Nicola saw, all too well, what was in his eyes. And what was in them, she saw, was anger. 'But I wonder if I oughtn't be asking the same of you. What can you be thinking, agreeing to marry that bounder?'

Nicola sucked in her breath. She ought to have known it was coming. Still, she hadn't expected him to be quite that up-front about it.

'If it is Lord Sebastian to whom you are referring in that

rude manner, Mr Sheridan,' she said haughtily, 'then the answer to your question – not, of course, that it is any of your business – is that I happen to love him. And he loves me.'

'Does he?' Nathaniel asked in a cold voice, a single eyebrow raised. 'Does he indeed?'

Nicola, as shocked as if he'd slapped her, cried, 'Of course he does! Nat, really! Why on earth should he have asked me to marry him if he didn't?'

'I don't know,' Nathaniel said in the same chilly voice. 'Did he tell you so?'

'Did he tell me what?' Nicola was aware that Stella Ashton wasn't the only one in the room who was looking at them curiously. Several people nearby had broken off their own conversations and were staring at Nicola, who'd been unable to keep her voice from rising to tremulous levels, she was so outraged. Madame Vieuxvincent, she knew, would object, as ladies never made scenes. But under the circumstances, Nicola felt she was justified.

'That he loved you,' Nathaniel said, with obviously forced patience.

Nicola longed with every fibre of her being to snap that he had – that he'd told her so a hundred times a day since their engagement. But of course the truth was that Lord Sebastian was quite casual, as far as lovers went. He had never once mentioned the word *love* . . . at least in connection with Nicola. He loved his new hunter, eighteen hands high with a neck as curved as a swan's. And he loved his new taupe waistcoat, which Nicola had made for him out of some leftover material from an opera cape she'd been disassembling to turn into a charming little bed jacket.

But he had never once said he loved her.

But what did mere words matter between two people who

felt for one another the strong and undying attachment she and Lord Sebastian shared? He *showed* her he loved her in myriad ways. Wasn't the diamond engagement ring on her left hand proof enough of that?

But before she could utter any of this, Nathaniel said, very nastily indeed, 'So he hasn't said it. I thought as much. Ask him, Nicola – or, God forbid, ask yourself – why a man in Bartholomew's position would agree to marry a girl – an *orphaned* girl – with only a hundred pounds a year.'

She drew in an indignant breath. Why, Nathaniel sounded exactly like the Milksop!

'Go ahead,' Nathaniel said. 'I dare you. Ask him.'

'What do you suppose he's going to say? Obviously you know, or you wouldn't be so confident about it,' she sputtered furiously. 'Well, if you know something you aren't telling me, just say it. I can't imagine why you haven't done so already. You've never felt very squeamish about sparing my feelings before now.'

This last remark caused, for some reason, a muscle Nicola had never before noticed to leap in Nathaniel's jaw.

'Fine,' he said. 'You don't want your feelings spared? Then ask your light o' love about Pease.'

'Peas?' Nicola echoed. 'What on earth do garden vegetables have to do with Lord Sebastian?'

'Not peas the vegetable,' Nathaniel scoffed. 'Pease the name. Ask your precious Lord Sebastian about Edward Pease, and see what he has to say.'

'And who,' Nicola demanded, 'is Edward Pease?'

'Lord Sebastian will tell you,' Nathaniel said knowingly. 'That is, if he's even half the man you seem to think he is.'

'He'll tell me,' Nicola said with a confidence she didn't feel. 'Lord Sebastian tells me everything. There isn't a single secret between us. We are both of us open as blank pages.'

'Then you haven't anything to worry about,' Nathaniel said. 'Have you?'

'No,' Nicola responded haughtily. 'I haven't. I'm happy as a lark.'

'I couldn't,' Nathaniel said, 'be more pleased to hear it. Don't forget to ask him.'

'About Edward Pease,' Nicola said. 'I won't. I'll ask him tonight. Or at the very least, first thing in the morning.'

'Fine,' Nathaniel said. 'You do that.'

'Fine,' she said. 'I will.'

'Fine,' he said.

'Fine,' she said.

Then, realizing that they could conceivably go on in that manner for hours, Nicola spun around and began to stalk from the room. She hadn't got very far, however, before her gaze fell upon Stella Ashton, who was still staring at her with a dumbfounded look upon her pretty face.

Nicola, though she would have liked to have made as dramatic an exit as possible, could not keep herself from pausing and turning toward the other girl to whisper, 'Really, Miss Ashton, but that shade of yellow doesn't suit you at all. *Do* dye that gown another colour. A nice rich burgundy or blue would do very nicely, I think.'

Then, before Stella could utter a word, Nicola darted from the room, to flee as quickly as she could the penetrating gaze of Eleanor's brother.

Nine

'Who is Edward Pease?' Nicola asked the next morning at the breakfast table.

Lord Farelly, who'd been buttering a piece of toast, promptly dropped both his knife and the toast, eliciting from him a curse that burned the ears of all the ladies present.

'Jarvis!' Lady Farelly cried. 'Really! Such language, and at breakfast, of all places.'

Lord Farelly, looking very red in the face, muttered an apology, and accepted from a waiting footman a new knife before reaching for a new piece of toast.

'Now,' Lady Farelly said, 'where were we? Oh, yes. Honoria, my love, I was meaning to ask you. Was that gown you wore to Almack's last night a new one? Because I don't think I've ever seen it before. I know you had one in a similar shade, but it was trimmed with ostrich feathers, I thought, and not gold braid.'

'It's the same gown, Mama,' Honoria said lightly, as she spooned a bit of sugar into her coffee. 'Nicola felt the feathers were too much, and would detract from my natural beauty.'

'Really?' Lady Farelly looked surprised. 'Well, Miss Sparks, I must congratulate you. The gold braid was a definite improvement.'

'Thank you, my lady,' Nicola said politely.

But the politeness was feigned. Nicola was not actually feeling very polite at all. She was not unaware that her question had not been answered. Not only had it not been answered, it had been quite firmly ignored . . . swept under the rug, one might even say, like the crumbs from Lord Farelly's dropped piece of toast.

Stuff, Nicola thought, *and bother.*

Up until that moment, she'd put down the Edward Pease remark as nonsense, something Nathaniel had invented on the spur of the moment, due to his extreme jealousy of Lord Sebastian – not, of course, that Nicola suspected Nathaniel of feeling anything for her but the same sort of brotherly affection he felt for Eleanor; but what young man wouldn't be jealous of Lord Sebastian, who was a living god?

Now she could not help wondering just what, exactly, it was that he knew. Obviously he knew something. He had not pulled the name Edward Pease out of nowhere. Not if it elicited that kind of response from Lord Farelly.

Only where had he heard it? And how had he come to connect it with her and the God?

It was no use, Nicola knew, asking Eleanor, whose head was filled with Sir Hugh, and nothing but Sir Hugh. And pride kept Nicola from asking Nathaniel if he'd mind elaborating. He'd told her to ask Lord Sebastian, and she had.

Except that, when she'd posed the question, he alone at the table – well, excepting Honoria – had gone right on eating, quite as if he hadn't the slightest idea what she was talking about.

Later that morning, as he stood preparing to go for his daily ride, Nicola sidled up to her fiancé and asked, after first making sure they were well out of earshot of the God's parents, 'Lord Sebastian? I was wondering . . . *do* you know who Edward Pease is?'

Tugging on his gloves, the God grinned fondly down at her. Nicola did not think she could be mistaken in this. The God positively looked fond of her.

And certainly the kisses the two of them shared – only one a day, for propriety's sake, and that one only before they were each ready to retire for their separate bedrooms for the evening – seemed quite fond, as well. Whatever else Nathaniel might think, clearly Lord Sebastian was not marrying her against his will. He *did* like her. At least a little.

'Pease again?' he asked, reaching out to give one of Nicola's glossy black curls, which had escaped from her coiffure, a tug. 'Never heard of the fellow. What's he been doing? Not trying to steal my girl, I hope.'

Nicola felt a flood of relief course through her. He didn't know. She was quite positive of that. Lord Sebastian hadn't the slightest idea who Edward Pease was. So Nathaniel was wrong.

Except . . .

Except Nathaniel Sheridan was never wrong. Well, about people, of course, he was often quite wrong. Look how wrong he was about the God. But Nathaniel Sheridan tended not to be wrong about things like this.

It was only this fact that caused Nicola to do what she did next. And that was claim, a little bit after Lord Sebastian had left the house, to have a megrim, and retire to her bed.

Nicola was rarely, if ever, ill, so her headache was a cause for some concern in the Bartholomew household. Lady Farelly offered very nicely to put off her dress-fitting appointment and stay by Nicola's bedside, in case she needed ice chips or something. And Lady Honoria insisted she would not go to her picnic outing with Philippa and Celestine Adams, not while Nicola was unwell. She too would stay at her dear friend's side during her time of need.

Nicola, though touched by this sisterly gesture, was at the same time mightily vexed by it. For of course if both Lady Farelly and Honoria stayed by her bedside, she could not do what she had invented the headache for in the first place.

And so she begged the ladies of the house to go about with their original plans . . . that she intended only to sleep. If she needed ice chips, Nicola informed them, she could send Martine for them. It would only distress her more to know that Lady Honoria and her mother were putting off their plans for her . . .

It took some doing, but in the end, Nicola was finally able to convince them to leave her. The moment she heard the front door close, Nicola leaped up from her bed, giving Martine, who really had started to go for ice chips, quite a start.

'It's all right, Martine,' Nicola informed her maid, as she bent to lace up her slippers. 'I'm right as rain. But be a love, will you, and whistle if you hear anyone coming back, particularly Lord Farelly?'

Martine, very much shocked at her mistress's behaviour, said she would do no such thing, and was in general being quite troublesome, until Nicola gave her a sovereign and told her to mind her own business. After that, Martine retired to a corner with her sewing box and a grim expression, muttering in French about little girls who stuck their noses where they didn't belong getting them cut off.

Nicola, though she understood French perfectly well, ignored her maid, and slipped from her bedchamber with the full intention of sticking her nose exactly where it didn't belong . . . namely, Lord Farelly's private study. She wasn't at all certain what she expected to find there, but if ever there was a place where she might find a clue as to the identity of Edward Pease, she supposed that was it. Lord Farelly had clearly heard of the man, even if his son had not, and it was possible Mr Pease and he had corresponded, and that that correspondence might even now lie openly on his lordship's desk, where Nicola might happen accidentally to spy it.

Snooping, of course, and eavesdropping of any kind were activities greatly frowned upon by Madame Vieuxvincent. And Nicola wouldn't have stooped to either of them if Lord Farelly had troubled himself to answer her question.

But as he'd seen fit to avoid the subject altogether, and not very subtly, Nicola felt she might snoop without compunction.

Still, as she padded lightly down the carpeted hallway leading to Lord Farelly's study, Nicola could not help glancing anxiously over her shoulder several times, alert for lurking footmen or housemaids. She encountered none, however, and when at last she laid her hand upon the latch, was able to slip into the mahogany-panelled room quite without being observed.

Lord Farelly had left for his office on Bond Street directly following breakfast . . . and Nicola's pointed question. His study, which also doubled as the family library, smelled pungently of the pipe his lordship liked to smoke when he was alone. The walls were lined with books and the occasional portrait of past Bartholomews. None of his ancestors even came close to having been as blessed by nature as Lord Sebastian had been. In fact, the family seemed to run rather strongly to fat. The earl, at least, was no lightweight.

But, Nicola reminded herself, she wasn't there to muse over how her future husband might look twenty years from now. She was there to snoop.

And so, accordingly, Nicola commenced snooping.

There was an art to rifling through someone else's drawers without leaving any indication that one had done so. Nicola was an old hand at such tricks, as it had generally been left to her to rifle through Madame Vieuxvincent's desk drawers when the need for sustenance, in the form of midnight raids of the larder, necessitated obtaining the key to the kitchen door. No matter how many times, and in whatever ingenious place, Madame Vieuxvincent hid this key, Nicola found it. And when the next morning, as Cook was crying over her missing chocolate gâteau, Madame demanded to know who had committed such an affront, Nicola had always been equally capable of uttering a bland denial. She had never once been caught, and rather doubted she'd ever been seriously suspected, either. She was, as it turned out, a master thief.

It wasn't long before she knew victory in her current quest, as well. Midway through his lordship's middle desk drawer, Nicola found a bundle of letters from none other than Mr Edward Pease himself. Settling in for an afternoon of reading, Nicola curled up beneath the earl's desk, so that any maid who happened to enter the study for some casual dusting would not discover her.

What Nicola read confused and disturbed her. Mr Edward Pease, it soon became apparent, worked for a company called Stockton and Darlington. Interestingly, Stockton and Darlington were towns not far from Beckwell Abbey.

More interestingly, Mr Pease seemed as fascinated by and interested in trains as Lord Farelly was. Most of his correspondence had to do with experiments in locomotion, such as the steam engines being used to haul coal in collieries. Such locomotives, according to Mr Pease, could pull the weight in coal of ten cart horses, and do it time and time again, without resting between deliveries of its load, as horses needed to.

Soon Nicola knew more about steam locomotives than she had ever cared to know about much of anything. How anyone could go on and on in such a vein about a machine – even a very revolutionary and new one – she couldn't understand. Lord Farelly, given his feelings about locomotives, undoubtedly found the whole thing highly fascinating, but Nicola was bored after only the second paragraph.

And, for all the trouble she'd taken, she'd found nothing at all that referred to her. Not a mention of her name, or any connection at all that might warrant Nathaniel's assertion that there was something suspicious about Lord Sebastian's affection for her.

As for Edward Pease, why, he was only a man who apparently shared Lord Farelly's great enthusiasm for locomotives; that was all.

Nicola was pleased – and at the same time a little disgusted with herself that Nathaniel had made her doubt the God. Worse, he'd made her doubt her own judgment, and *that* was upsetting. Nicola was shuffling the letters back into the order in which she'd found them when a small slip of paper fell from the pile and onto the carpet. She picked it up and was about, without so much as a glance at it, to stick it back into the pile where she thought it belonged, when something about it caught her eye.

It was a torn piece of foolscap, smaller than all the other pages. Only instead of writing upon it, there was a drawing. At first Nicola could make nothing of it. She turned the slip of paper this way and that, squinting at it. It looked somehow familiar, and yet she could not tell how.

And then it hit her. The squiggly line down the middle of the page was the river Tweed. She knew that river as well as she knew how to add bunting to an Easter bonnet. It was the exact river into which the stream that burbled by Beckwell Abbey – the same stream the Milksop had once tried to keep her from swimming in – flowed into. She was looking, she realized, at a map of the Northumberland region . . . her home.

But while she recognized the river Tweed, she could not understand what the rest of the markings on the paper indicated. Killingworth Colliery – she recognized it by its place on the river – was marked with an X, and from that X extended a line that wound along beside the river, hatched every eighth of an inch like a ladder. The line seemed to wind right through the place on the map where Beckwell Abbey would be located, if the mapmaker had bothered to draw it in. It went straight along until it ran into Stockton, a town some miles away from Beckwell Abbey.

Except that whoever had drawn the map – and Nicola supposed it could only have been Edward Pease, the author of all the letters in the pile she still held – had left off the abbey. Or perhaps he was confused. Because no such road – if that *was* a road, indicated by the hatch-marked line – existed between Killingworth and Stockton.

And then, as Nicola sat there, turning the map this way and that, trying to make sense of it, it hit her.

That hatch-marked line wasn't a road. Not a *proper* road, anyhow.

It was a *railway*.

Nicola was convinced of it. It looked so very like the track on which the *Catch Me Who Can* had run.

And the track ran straight through the middle of Beckwell Abbey.

So absorbed was she in the map that Nicola hadn't heard footsteps beyond the study door. In fact, she wasn't aware that she was not alone until she heard a cough. Crouched beneath his lordship's desk, Nicola immediately froze, hardly daring even to breathe.

Straining her ears, since the desk blocked her from looking out, Nicola tried to determine who had entered the room. If it was one of the maids, or Jennings, the butler, Nicola would be all right.

But if it was Lord Farelly, and he attempted to sit down at his desk, and discovered Nicola there where his feet should go, she was, she knew, in very deep trouble.

Someone coughed again. And then Nicola heard, 'Ah, there it is. I told him he musta left it. I'll be sworn, he'd lose his head if it weren't sewn on.'

The back of Nicola's neck prickled with relief. It was only Mrs Steadman, the housekeeper. Nicola, peeking out from behind the desk, saw her bustling from the room, holding one of the God's evening coats beneath her arm. Lord Sebastian must have left it behind accidentally the other night when his father had had him in for a brandy before bed.

The study door closed firmly behind the housekeeper, and Nicola, alone again, was able to breathe freely once more. Hastily, she tucked the letters back where she'd found them. Climbing to her feet, she cast a swift glance around the room, wanting to make sure she'd left it as she'd found it. She saw nothing amiss. The only thing Lord Farelly might find different upon his return was his map, which would be missing. That was because Nicola had slipped it up her sleeve. The earl would surely wonder where it had disappeared to, but Nicola doubted she'd ever fall suspect of removing it. That was because she was, after all, a lady.

A lady who had a call to make, and at once, megrim or no.

Ten

He was late.

Nicola supposed she couldn't blame him. It wasn't as if, given their last meeting – or next-to-last meeting, as she supposed it had happened to be – he had much of an incentive, or possibly even desire, to see her.

Still, it was rude to leave a lady waiting. Particularly a lady who hadn't any sort of escort, and who was, with every passing moment, running the very grave danger of discovery. For if Lady Honoria – or, Lord forbid, her mother – should happen to arrive home before Nicola made it back, and found her gone, she would have some serious explaining to do. Ladies did not arrange surreptitious assignations with gentlemen in public parks . . . even with gentlemen to whom they might happen to be related.

'Spare a penny, miss?'

Nicola started. An old woman, wearing a heavy shawl about her head and shoulders – much too heavy, Nicola thought, given the late-afternoon warmth – stood beside the bench Nicola was seated upon, holding out a gnarled hand.

'A ha'penny?' the old woman asked hopefully. 'Anything to spare, dearie?'

Nicola, her heart still drumming rapidly – given what had happened the last time she'd ventured into this very park, she thought it not at all unusual that she should feel so nervous – opened her reticule, found a penny, and laid it in the old woman's hand.

'Lord bless you,' the crone – for she *was* one, badly in need of a bit of cleaning up; had Nicola not been staying with the Bartholomews, she might have brought the woman home, and attempted it, for Nicola loved a project – said, and moved on to the couple occupying the next bench – a couple whom Nicola could not help noticing had either done a very good job of escaping their chaperone, or had just recently married, as they seemed unable to keep their hands to themselves, but instead were placing them all over one another. She had carefully chosen this bench because it was out of sight of the carriage path. Unfortunately, she was not alone in being desirous of such solitude. Thank goodness she and the God had a little more self-control than *some* people . . .

'Nicola?'

Nicola jumped about a mile in the air, then, flattening a hand to her chest, turned and chastised her cousin.

'You're late,' she said. 'And you frightened me half to death.'

Looking churlish, and without waiting to ask permission, the Milksop lowered himself upon Nicola's bench, flipping the tails of his sage-green coat out from behind him as he did so.

'I was holding a winning hand at whist,' the Milksop said irritably, 'at my club when your message came. Did you expect me to just throw down my cards?' He made a face. 'Don't answer that. Knowing you, I think I already know the answer.'

Nicola was not hurt. Nothing the Milksop could say could hurt her. She was, truth be told, more offended by his person than his attitude toward her. While the coat of sage green might, on anyone else, have looked passable, Harold had chosen to pair it with a tartan – *tartan* – waistcoat, and red – *red* – breeches. Even at Christmastime, Nicola would not have approved of such an outfit. She wondered, not for the first time, if perhaps the Milksop suffered from colourblindness.

'Would you mind telling me,' Harold wanted to know, 'what was so all-fired important that you had to drag me from my club to meet you in all this secrecy, and in such a dreadfully out-of-the-way place?'

'Yes,' Nicola said. 'I mean, no, I don't mind telling you. I mean . . . '

'Spare a penny, sir?'

The Milksop looked up and, just as Nicola had, started at the sight of the beggarwoman. Only unlike Nicola, he did not reach immediately into his pocket. Instead he said, 'Ye gods, woman, what are you about, pawing me like that? Get away with you, or I shall call a Bow Street Runner and have you arrested for vagrancy.'

The old woman hurried away, muttering beneath her breath. Nicola thought – again, not for the first time – how much she despised her cousin Harold. Then, guiltily remembering that her own fiancé had reacted very much the same way to a much more appealing beggar, she reminded herself how vexing it was to constantly be approached with requests to share one's own hard-earned coin.

'What is the name of the man who wished to buy the abbey?' she demanded without further preamble, in an effort to put a quick end to their interview.

Harold turned to stare at her as if she were as demented as the poor creature whom he had just sent scurrying away. 'You brought me all the way down here to ask me *that*?'

'Yes,' Nicola said. 'Who was it?'

'Edward somebody. Oh, that's right. Pease. Edward Pease.' The Milksop's gaze roved toward the couple on the bench beside theirs. 'Good Lord,' he said. 'What's going on *here*?'

'Never mind that,' Nicola said. Her heart had seemed to give a spasm at his words – his first words, not the part about the kissing couple – as if an unseen hand had reached inside her chest, taken hold of that organ and squeezed. Edward Pease. Edward Pease was the man who'd made the offer for her home. Edward Pease, who seemed to want to put a railway between Killingworth and Stockton. The only thing standing in his way, it seemed, was Beckwell Abbey, and her unwillingness to sell it.

'Why all this interest in Pease all of a sudden?' Harold asked. Then his piggy eyes lit up. 'Did you change your mind, then, about selling? Is that it? Want Father to contact the man, and go ahead with the sale? Because you've only to say the word, Nicola, and he'll do it for you. Father doesn't hold a grudge for the shabby way you've treated me. Though that's partly due to me, since I, of course, refrained from telling him the whole of your disgraceful behaviour.'

Nicola, feeling the map in her sleeve, where she'd left it, said nothing. So it was true. That was all she could think. Everything Nathaniel had said was true. Harold, too, now that she thought of it. He'd said a fellow like the Viscount Farnsworth could never love a girl like Nicola. And it appeared he'd been right. Clearly the God was marrying her only out of some design of his father's, a friend of Edward Pease's, in order to help him get his hands on the abbey.

But no. It couldn't be. Nicola thought back to all the happy times she and Lord Sebastian had shared. No, it wasn't possible. It couldn't have all been feigned. The God had to like her a little. Even the most controlling parent couldn't force his son to propose to a girl he didn't like. Sebastian *had* to like her. He just *had* to. That part about Beckwell Abbey and Edward Pease . . . well, surely that was only a coincidence. Surely that was all it was.

Hardly knowing what she was doing, Nicola stood up and, without another word, began walking away. She was going, she supposed, back to the Bartholomews', but she did not consciously think of this until the Milksop reached out and seized her by the wrist.

'Nicola,' he said. 'Where are you going? What's wrong with you? You send me running all the way down here to ask me some stupid fellow's name, and then that's it? You just leave me here?'

'I'm sorry, Harold,' Nicola said dazedly. 'I – I suppose I'm not feeling very well just now. I . . . I think I had better go home.'

The Milksop looked torn between indignation and concern. He was still put out with her for what he considered her ill-treatment of him, but even he had to admit that, with her face suddenly drained of all colour, she did not seem, just then, in her usual fighting form.

'Nicola,' he said. 'Let me see you home, at least.'

Nicola didn't want him to – knowing the Milksop, he would probably invite himself for supper – but as she really did feel very strange indeed, she allowed him to tuck her into his carriage and drive her back to the Bartholomews' . . . where she found, much to her consternation, both Lady Farelly and her daughter had preceded her home. They looked quite surprised that Nicola, who'd been in bed with a megrim when last they'd seen her, should have ventured outside, and with none other than the Milksop, whom she'd made no secret of detesting.

Nicola, even ill as she felt over her dreadful – and very confusing – discovery, was able to rally her spirits enough to think up a really capital lie to cover for her seemingly odd behaviour. She told the ladies of the house that, having recovered from her headache, she'd remembered that she had something most pressing to discuss with her cousin, and that he'd very kindly met her in the park . . . where her megrim had unfortunately returned with a vengeance.

Both ladies seemed to find this monstrous lie quite believable. They urged Nicola to return to bed, which she did gladly, leaving the Milksop to the ministrations of the ladies Farelly. Things had become entirely too complicated too quickly for Nicola, and she honestly did feel ill. Madame Vieuxvincent, for all her careful teachings, had never said anything about how her pupils were to proceed in a situation such as this one.

Once safely ensconced in her room, Nicola allowed Martine to fuss over her, until, satisfied her mistress was comfortable, the maid withdrew to her own room, with the admonition that this time, Nicola stay abed.

Nicola was only too happy to oblige. She lay for nearly an hour beneath the bedcovers, staring unseeingly up at the filmy white canopy above her head. It couldn't be true, was all she could think. It simply couldn't. The God *had* to love her. He *had* to!

But supposing he didn't? Supposing Nathaniel was right? And Eleanor. What was it Eleanor had said? 'What is the viscount like as a person?'

Nicola had to confess that, given this new, startling information, she couldn't, in all honesty, say. Or rather, she could: the viscount was the kind of man who wouldn't hesitate to strike an orphan in the head with his cane . . . or rob her of her only birthright.

No. No, she simply couldn't believe that. Not of Lord Sebastian. Not of the God!

All Nicola was sure of was that she couldn't possibly marry a man who didn't love her. No, not even the God. Some girls, she knew, might go ahead with the wedding, even suspecting what Nicola was beginning to suspect. Some girls, Nicola supposed, would convince themselves they could *make* their husbands love them.

But what kind of marriage was that? That was not what Romeo and Juliet had, or Tristan and Isolde, or Lochinvar and his beloved Ellen. Guenevere had been quite sure of the love of both Arthur *and* Lancelot. Although Nicola had never liked Guenevere, who had always seemed a bit feckless, she had, at least, identified with her much more than she'd ever identified with the lily maid of Astolat, who had died of unrequited love of Lancelot.

Now, suddenly, Nicola found she had a good deal more in common with that poor creature than she'd ever had with the queen of Camelot.

It was ridiculous. It was unconscionable. That *this* was what came of being a thistle, blown about by life . . . well, Nicola wouldn't stand for it. She was no lily maid of Astolat meekly to perish in the face of rejection. And she was no fickle-minded Guenevere, either. She was, she decided, much more like Joan of Arc, who unfortunately hadn't lived long enough to have a love affair . . . at least, not one that had been recorded.

But she had, of course, fought in a war. Which was precisely, Nicola decided, what this was. War.

And so, an hour after she'd been tucked into bed by her maid, Nicola threw back the bedclothes and leaped from it, prepared to gird for battle. It was no joke dressing by herself, as she dared not ring for Martine, whom she knew would only rebuke her for getting up. But Nicola managed all the stays and hooks and hairpins on her own, and when she inspected the result in the mirror, she found it adequate, if not particularly glamorous.

Then, striding across the room, she threw open her bed-chamber door, stepped across the hallway, and started down the stairs.

She found him, as she'd known she would, at the bagatelle table in the library. He glanced up as she walked in, and said, 'Oh, there you are. Mama said you were feeling a bit under the weather. Better now? Are you going to the opera tonight with us? I hope you will; you know how deadly dull I find it. I'll need you to nudge me awake if I nod off during the boring bits.'

Nicola did not reply to any of this. Instead she stood there with her hands at her sides – though really, in her mind's eye, she was holding both lance and staff – and said, 'Lord Sebastian. I need to know. Do you love me?'

The God, who'd been leaning across the bagatelle table to make a difficult shot, looked up at her from beneath those long, golden eyelashes. 'What?' he asked in a tone that was part amusement and part incredulity.

'It's a simple enough question,' Nicola said. 'Do . . . you . . . love . . . me?'

The God straightened and, reaching for a piece of chalk, applied it to the tip of his bagatelle cue. The whole of the time, he did not take his blue-eyed gaze off Nicola.

'I'm marrying you, aren't I?' he said, a distinct upward tilt to the corners of his lips.

'That's not an answer,' Nicola said.

The tilt disappeared. The God laid down the chalk and said, 'Say, what *is* this? Pre-wedding jitters? Don't tell me you're thinking of backing out, Nicola. I'd look a right great chump in front of the other fellows if you did.'

'I asked you a simple question,' Nicola said unsmilingly. 'And you still haven't given me an answer. Do you love me, Lord Sebastian, or don't you?'

'Why, of course I love you,' the God said in a wounded tone. 'Though I must say, I've liked you better than I do just now. Whatever is the matter with you?'

'Why?'

'Well, because you're normally such a happy sort, and just now you seem rather out of sorts.'

'No,' Nicola said, with a glance at the ceiling as if for strength. 'I mean, why do you love me?'

'Why do I . . . ?' The God gave a laugh. Nicola wasn't certain, but it sounded to her a bit uneasy. 'Why does any fellow love a girl?' he asked.

'I don't know,' Nicola said. 'And I don't particularly care. I'm asking why *you* love *me*.'

'I say, Nicola,' the God said, finally laying down his bagatelle cue. 'Are you quite all right? You seem a bit . . . '

'What is it about me, my lord' – Nicola would not relent – 'that you love?'

The God, looking exceedingly uncomfortable now, ran a hand through his thick blond hair and peered at her curiously in the last rays of the setting sun, which were streaming into the room from the stained-glass window just behind him. The light, coming in through the coloured panes, stained the carpet beneath their feet a myriad of colours, blood red, Nicola could not help noticing, being foremost among them.

'Well,' the God said. 'I suppose I love you because normally – when you aren't acting like you are now – you're a . . . well, you're a jolly sort of girl.'

'I'm jolly,' Nicola echoed. 'You love me because I am jolly.'

'Well, yes,' the God said, seeming to warm to the subject now that he'd got the initial words out. 'You laugh a lot. I mean, most days.'

'Because I am so jolly,' Nicola said.

'Right. And you aren't afraid to try new things. Like the *Catch Me Who Can*, for instance. Not many girls would have ridden on that thing, but you didn't blink an eye. I liked that.' He smiled at her, a charming smile. The same smile that, the day before, would have sent Nicola's heartstrings fluttering.

Today, it hardly caused them to stir.

'You love me,' Nicola said, 'and want to marry me, and live with me for ever, until one or the other of us dies, because I am jolly, and I was not afraid to ride the *Catch Me Who Can*.'

The God considered this statement with some gravity. Then, after a moment's reflection, he added tentatively, 'And because you're pretty?' as if it were a quiz, and he wasn't certain of the right answer.

Nicola, however, ignored this, as it was entirely unworthy of notice.

'Would it surprise you to know,' Nicola asked, 'that I consider love a sacred thing that transcends definition, capable of bringing out both the best and the worst of human nature? Historically, men have performed great, life-risking feats in the name of love. They have also committed crimes of unspeakable horror, for the very same reason. I highly doubt, Lord Sebastian, that, given what I've just heard, what you feel for me falls under this definition.'

The God's perfectly formed mouth fell open. He seemed quite astonished, as if one of his mother's footmen, instead of setting a bowl of soup before him, had placed there instead a hissing snake.

'Would you be willing to die for me, my lord?' Nicola asked. 'Would you forfeit your life for mine? No, I rather think not. Men don't tend to sacrifice themselves for women they find *jolly*. When I love – and you will note that I say *when*, as I do not believe, as of this moment, that what I felt for you, my lord, was love . . . not real, undying love, such as a woman feels for a man, what, just for instance, Desdemona felt for Othello, or Cleopatra for Mark Antony – it will be forever, and it will not be because of the way someone looks, or whether or not he happens to make me laugh, but because we share a common view of life and all of its vagaries, forming a unique and indefinable bond between us. When we are separated even for a moment, our very beings cry out in torment, until we are once again reunited. And I would willingly die a thousand deaths to keep him from suffering even one.

'That,' Nicola concluded, 'is what love is, Lord Sebastian, and that is not, unfortunately, what you and I share. Therefore, I find that, much to my regret, I cannot possibly marry you. I'm sure you understand.'

And, turning around, Nicola strode quickly and quietly from the room, not stopping when Lord Sebastian, behind her, cried, 'Nicola! Nicola, wait!'

She kept going. She did not stop even when Lady Farelly, coming down the hallway just as Nicola exited the library, cried, 'Miss Sparks! Whatever are you doing out of bed?'

No, Nicola did not stop, not even as she headed toward the front door, which, much to the consternation of the butler, Nicola threw open and walked through. She did not stop until she had walked all the way to Eleanor's house, several streets away, and had come to the door, and rung the bell.

A housemaid in a white mobcap opened the door, looking a good deal surprised to see a caller at such an unconventional hour, well past tea, but not yet time for supper. Nicola asked her if Lady Sheridan was at home, to which the maid replied that she'd see.

But fortunately Lady Sheridan happened to be close by, and when she heard Nicola's voice, she went to the door, shooed the maid aside, and, looking down at her daughter's most particular friend with great surprise, cried, 'Nicola! Whatever are you doing out by yourself, and at this hour? Did you come by carriage? Surely you didn't walk all this way alone. Are you quite all right, my dear? Is something wrong?'

To which Nicola replied by flinging her arms around Lady Sheridan's neck and bursting into tears.

Part 2

Eleven

There was nothing in the world – at least the world as it existed in 1808 – quite as irreparably damaging to a woman's reputation as a failed marriage. The only thing that came even remotely close to the shame and degradation of such a disaster was a broken engagement. Madame Vieuxvincent had warned her girls most strenuously on the subject, urging them to think very, very hard before breaking off a betrothal, as such an action could result not only in public humiliation, but also actual court action. Some jilted lovers were not above suing the parties who dropped them for breach of promise.

What Madame ought to have instructed her pupils in, Nicola could not help thinking now, was not the dangers of breaking off an engagement, but the dangers of entering imprudently into one in the first place.

For she might have avoided the current situation in which she found herself had she stopped to think, even for a moment, what marriage to the God might actually be like. In the girlish daze into which his proposal had thrown her, she'd been incapable of thinking of anything save the ermine she would wear once she became viscountess, and how nice it was going to be when finally she was allowed to touch Lord Sebastian's eyelashes, as a wife, by her station, had every right to.

She had never stopped to think how little the two of them, she and the God, had in common. She had never wondered, *What will we discuss over the table at suppertime?* Really, the God but rarely spoke at all at mealtimes, except to ask for the butter, or occasionally to tell a long and, to Nicola's ears, frightfully boring story about a horse he had or had not happened to bet upon. Certainly the God was, upon these occasions, terribly nice to look at. But his conversation was somewhat wanting. He could not even be trusted to know a single current event, as he opened a newspaper but rarely, and then only to look at the sporting pages. And heaven knew he had never read a single novel, much less a collection of poetry.

Why Nicola had not thought of any of these things before accepting his marriage proposal, she could not fathom. She only knew that there was no possible way she could marry the viscount after all.

And so she had set out for the safest place she could think of – the arms of Lady Sheridan, who had always been so kind to her and from which she hadn't the slightest inclination to stir. Instead, after Eleanor and her mother soothed and petted her enough to get the full story out, Nicola sent, with a footman, word to Martine that she was to pack immediately and join Nicola at the Sheridans'.

Further, and with Lady Sheridan's help, Nicola sent an apologetic note to Lady Farelly, thanking her for her hospitality, but explaining that a marriage between Nicola and the viscount was quite impossible. She accompanied this note with the ring Lord Sebastian had given her. In this way was Nicola's engagement to the God finally put at an end.

Or so she hoped. It would be, of course, extremely tedious if Lord Sebastian chose to fight her on the subject. She didn't suppose he'd take her to court – she hadn't, after all, any sort of income to speak of, and for him to sue a penniless orphan, even one whose father had been a baron, would be looked upon most unsympathetically by the press.

Still, Nicola expected a reprisal of some kind, and it came the very next morning, whilst she was still abed, having sat awake most of the night with streaming eyes and a throbbing head – apparently the Lord was punishing her for lying about having a megrim the day before by giving her a real one.

Eleanor was the one to bring the bad news . . . Eleanor, who had, in her role as loyal friend, of course absolutely agreed with Nicola's action of breaking off the engagement. A man whose only spoken words of love to his intended were to inform her that he found her jolly was no sort of man at all, to Eleanor's way of thinking. She, like Nicola, was quite bitterly disappointed in the God . . .

And all the more so the next morning, when, as Eleanor hurried to warn Nicola, he came to call, demanding to see his former fiancée and insisting that no one or nothing should keep him from her . . . although in point of fact Nathaniel and two of the footmen were currently doing so, having barred the viscount's access to the stairs leading to the guest room in which Nicola was staying.

'He looks a good deal upset,' Eleanor informed her friend. 'Quite wild, as a matter of fact. I would venture his cravat hasn't seen an iron this morning.'

'I suppose he's probably frantic because his father's threatened to cut him off,' Nicola said bitterly into her pillow.

'Why should his father have done that?' Eleanor wondered.

But of course Nicola could not tell her that . . . not about

Mr Pease, and the Stockton and Darlington Company's plan to expand their railway enterprise right through the centre of Beckwell Abbey. The fact that the viscount had tried to marry her without loving her in the least was bad enough. But if people learned *why* he'd wanted to marry her – for Nicola was certain Nathaniel was right, and that Lord Farelly was somehow involved in a scheme with Mr Pease to get his hands on her home – it would simply be too humiliating to bear.

Besides, it was all over now. Nicola was safe. So why bring it up?

'I don't know,' Nicola said, biting her lip. 'I'm just being silly, I suppose.'

'Oh. Still, Nicola,' Eleanor said worriedly. 'I wonder if you oughtn't see him. I don't think he quite understands that it's over between you.'

'I sent back the ring,' Nicola pointed out. 'How much plainer can I make it?'

But it appeared that even so obvious a gesture as the return of an engagement ring was not enough to convince Lord Sebastian that all was well and truly finished between himself and Nicola. As the next few days passed, and Nicola began slowly to recover from her humiliation at his hands, the viscount did not let up in his pursuit of her, coming to call at least thrice daily – despite being turned away, each and every time, without ever once seeing Nicola. As if stationing himself in the Sheridans' downstairs parlour were not enough, he also sent bouquet after bouquet of roses, as if he hoped that Nicola might be overcome by the scent of so many flowers, and change her mind.

'You'll have to see him eventually,' Eleanor reminded her the first day Nicola felt up to dining with the rest of the family, and not in solitude in her room. 'I mean, you can't hide from him for the rest of the season. You're bound to see one another at Almack's, at the very least.'

'I know,' Nicola said. Martine – who in typically French fashion did not see what the problem was with a loveless marriage, and who was quite put out by the fact that her mistress would not be a viscountess after all – was being particularly savage with Nicola's thick black curls, causing Nicola to cry, 'Ow! Have a care, Martine,' at regular intervals during her toilette.

'You ought at least to go down and tell him you haven't changed your mind,' Eleanor said. 'Then maybe he'll leave you alone for a bit. Unless, of course, you aren't really sure, and seeing him might set flame to your passion for him once more.'

'I assure you, Eleanor – ow! Martine, really, *must* you be so rough? – my passion for Lord Sebastian has completely flamed out. I just don't want to see him – or any of the Bartholomews – any time soon. Is that wrong of me?'

'I should say not,' Eleanor said loyally. And she went away to tell the viscount that Nicola still refused to see him.

There was one person, however, who came to call that Nicola could not refuse to see. And that was her guardian, Lord Renshaw.

'Oh, no,' Nicola moaned when she learned this. 'Not the Grouser! I wonder what *he* can want?'

But Nicola was fairly certain she knew what her guardian wanted. And so when she entered the drawing room where he was waiting to see her – a handkerchief held to his nose because all of the roses in the room, gifts from the viscount, were making him sneeze – she had her defence already well prepared.

'Never fear, my lord,' Nicola said lightly, as she swept into the room. 'I shall pay back, to the penny, the money you lent me for my trousseau. Indeed, I spent only a small portion of it, on silk orange blossoms for my wedding slippers. You may have the rest at once . . .'

The Grouser, his eyes red-rimmed, intoned from behind the handkerchief, 'I did not come here, you foolish girl, to speak to you about the money I lent you. I came to ask if you'd lost your senses.'

Nicola looked at her guardian in some surprise. She ought, she knew, to have expected an attack of the sort, as the Grouser was extremely old-fashioned and traditional. Still, she hadn't supposed that, aside from the money she'd wasted, Lord Renshaw would care much about her decision not to marry the viscount.

'I'm terribly sorry to have disappointed you, my lord,' Nicola said, a little affronted. 'But I would think you'd want me to marry a man who loved me. Lord Sebastian, as it happens, does not.'

'Love!' the Grouser cried, as if the word were very distasteful indeed. 'That's all girls like you ever think about. I suppose that's why you refused to marry my son. Because you didn't think him enough in love with you. This, I see, is what comes of an education. Ridiculous idea, educating women. They thrust those poets in front of you – this Byron fellow, and Wordsworth and Walter Scott – and fill your heads with nonsense about knights and love matches. Well, I'm sorry to disappoint you, Nicola, but there are no knights in real life, nor do love matches happen nearly as often as they do in books. In real life, Nicola, men and women marry because it is prudent . . . and it would have been exceedingly prudent for you to have married the Viscount Farnsworth.'

Stung, Nicola managed to keep her temper in check long enough to say, as mildly as she could, 'Prudent, perhaps, from a financial respect, my lord, but not so far as my heart was concerned.'

'Your heart.' The Grouser blew his nose noisily. 'What about your belly, young woman? Because I'm wondering how you think you are going to go on feeding it if you keep turning down suitor after suitor. One hundred pounds a year does not go far, and you won't always be able to depend upon your schoolmates' parents to feed and house you.'

Nicola narrowed her eyes at her guardian. Really, but he was a most odious creature. She didn't know what she'd done to deserve to be saddled with such an obnoxious relation.

'I can always,' Nicola said, far more sweetly than she felt, 'go back to Beckwell Abbey, can't I, my lord? Seeing as how I didn't sell it. Do you not think that, at least, was prudent of me, given the circumstances?'

The Grouser, having finally found a corner of the room far enough from the roses that he could breathe without sneezing, lowered his handkerchief and sent a glare in her direction.

'No, I most certainly do not,' he said quite angrily. 'You could live comfortably and well on twelve thousand pounds. Still can. The offer stands, you know. All you have to do is say the word, and—'

Nicola felt something bubble up inside of her. For once it wasn't laughter. No, it was anger, hot and dark.

'Sell the abbey?' Nicola's voice rose dangerously in both volume and tone. 'Sell my only home? Oh, that's rich. And I don't suppose you'd happen to know why your Mr Pease wants to buy the abbey, would you?'

The Grouser looked slightly taken aback. He had known, of course, that his ward had a temper – hadn't she once flown at him in a rage for suggesting it would be cheaper, in the long run, to have her aged pony put down than to keep feeding it the mashed oats its age and infirmity required? – but it had been some time since he'd seen her quite this angry.

'I'm sure I don't know,' the Grouser replied. 'And I hardly think it any of your business what the man chooses to do with something he has paid fair price for . . .'

'Run a train through it!' Nicola shouted. Yes, shouted, Madame Vieuxvincent's warnings against a lady raising her voice in the house – or anywhere, for that matter – be damned. 'That's what Mr Pease wants to do with Beckwell Abbey, run a railway straight through the middle of it!'

Lord Renshaw looked stunned. He stood with his hand-kerchief half-forgotten in his fingers, and simply stared at her.

'How do you think that's going to make the local farmers feel?' Nicola demanded, her voice continuing to ring out at decibels that would have shocked Madame excessively. 'Having great loads of coal thundering through their pastureland? Oh, I'm sure the sheep will like that very much!'

The Grouser, some of his astonishment seeming to ebb, eyed Nicola warily.

'Now, now,' he said, in tones Nicola assumed he thought soothing, but which, thanks to the roses, were quite the opposite, being phlegmy and unctuous. 'Now, now, my dear. I don't know where you heard this terrible rumour, but I assure you, it is all a mistake—'

'It isn't a mistake,' Nicola raged. 'It's perfectly true.' She had the map with her – indeed, she was rarely without it. She had taken to pulling it out often, whenever she felt her resolve against marrying Lord Sebastian needed bolstering.

For it was not easy, giving up a god . . . even a god who had treated her so shabbily.

She thought about pulling it out to show to Lord Renshaw. But that, she knew, would only lead to unpleasant questions as to how she'd come to obtain such a thing. It was one thing to break Madame's rule about shouting. It was quite another to rightfully be accused of both snooping and pilfering. And Nicola wasn't in a mood to hear her guardian chasten her for thievery.

'Allow me to assure you,' Nicola said, keeping the map safely inside her sleeve, where it had fit so snugly since she'd found it, 'that what I am telling you is true. You see now why I can never sell, don't you, my lord? Because while I have a breath in my body, Beckwell Abbey will remain standing.'

She thought for a moment that Lord Renshaw did see, that he was as horrified as she was over the idea of metal tracks being laid across the buttercup-dotted pastureland that surrounded her ancestral home. That he too could not stand the idea of a locomotive – a much, much larger one than the *Catch Me Who Can* – thundering through the middle of what had once been Beckwell Abbey's breakfast room, with its leaded glass in diamond-shaped panes, heavy oak beams, and flagstoned floor. That he was appalled as she was at the thought of the thick black smoke that hung over the Killingworth Colliery clouding the clear blue that canopied her childhood home, the most beautiful place, in her opinion, in the entire world. That he, too, understood the moral responsibility she had to protect, at all costs, these things that had been bequeathed her.

But then Lord Renshaw lifted his handkerchief once more to his thin nose and blew violently into it.

'You,' he said, through the once-white linen, 'are the most contrary girl I have ever had the misfortune to meet, Nicola

Sparks. Your absurd attachment for that dilapidated dung heap you call your home will, I am convinced, spell your doom. But if you choose to ruin your life, that is, of course, your prerogative.'

Before Nicola, still blinking over the 'dilapidated dung heap' comment, could reply, the Grouser added, 'Frankly, Nicola, I wash my hands of you. For an orphan, you were always impossibly spoiled, and I am sorry to see that all of that expensive schooling upon which you squandered your father's money did not improve you in the least.'

As Nicola stood and stared, her mouth slightly ajar – Madame would have been horrified: an open mouth was an abomination before the Lord – Lord Renshaw gave his nose a final, violent honk, then added, 'What your idiot father was thinking, leaving his estate to you and not to me, I cannot imagine.'

That did it. No one – no one – called Nicola's father names, and got away with it.

Nicola cried, with flashing eyes, 'I'll tell you what he was thinking. He was thinking he'd better not trust the thing he loved best in all the world to a man completely lacking in any sort of moral fibre or feeling!'

But Lord Renshaw, rather than being wounded to the quick, as she'd hoped, only rolled his eyes, tugged on his hat, and said, in a voice thick not only with phlegm, but venom, too, 'I want you to know, you ignorant girl, that whatever happens next, you have only yourself to blame.'

With that, the Grouser left the room.

And Nicola sank down amid the dozens of roses Lord Sebastian had left for her, her knees – but even more alarmingly, her spirit – seeming to give out beneath her.

Twelve

'Nicky?'

Nicola, curled onto a divan in the Sheridans' front parlour, looked up, startled.

'It's only me,' Nathaniel said, and sat down beside her. 'I heard the shouting. Are you all right?'

Nicola nodded wordlessly, not trusting herself to speak. She was trying to regain her composure after the very disturbing interview she'd just had with her guardian, but she feared she was not doing a very good job of it. Tears were pricking the corners of her eyes, and her nose felt a bit tingly. It seemed amazing to her that she could have any tears left, after the buckets she'd wept over losing Lord Sebastian. But apparently tears were one thing – unlike money and her guardian's patience with her – that could never run out.

She did not, however, relish the idea of weeping in front of Nathaniel Sheridan. Why could she not, as Madame had always urged, maintain at all times an air of cool disdain around this particular young man? She managed so admirably with others. Why not with Nathaniel?

Using the lace trim of one of her sleeves, she attempted to dab surreptitiously at her eyes, hoping he would not notice their dampness. But she apparently wasn't surreptitious

127

enough, since a moment later a clean white handkerchief dangled in front of her face.

'Go ahead,' Nathaniel said when she glanced at him. 'It's clean.'

Nicola had not expected anything else. Nathaniel, despite his love for mathematics and science, was not one of those untidy professorial types, but always maintained a neat and pleasing appearance. It had been one of the things that had irritated Nicola most about him – that he should look always so presentable, even handsome, while possessing such an infuriating personality. It made it entirely too hard to hate him, or even, as she had many of the other men in her life, to think up a suitable nickname for him. The Professor wasn't apt, and Abacus didn't fit, either. He remained simply, stubbornly Nathaniel in her mind.

'Thank you,' she said hesitantly. Then, taking the handkerchief, she attempted to erase whatever damage had been done to her face . . . though, even as she accepted his help and mopped herself up, she could not help but wonder just what, precisely, Nathaniel was doing, being so nice to her. It wasn't a bit like him.

Then she remembered that actually, of late he'd done any number of kind things for her. He'd saved her from having to dance the Sir Roger with the Milksop, for one, and warned her of Edward Pease – how had he known about him, anyway? – for another. Ever since Nicola had come to stay with the Sheridans, though she'd seen little of him, having kept mostly to her bed, Nathaniel had been performing little services for her, such as keeping Lord Sebastian out of the parts of the house she might likely venture into. Really, but he was being quite as conscientious as if she were, as she and Eleanor had often joked, his sister in truth. It was an oddly comforting feeling.

And Nicola needed a little comfort just then.

'I suppose,' Nathaniel said, when it appeared that Nicola had pulled herself together for conversation, 'that Lord Renshaw isn't too happy with you just now.'

'Not very,' Nicola said with a slight, humourless laugh. 'Not only won't I marry anyone he's picked out for me, but I won't make proper business decisions, either. He said he's quite washed his hands of me.'

'Well, I can't see how that's a bad thing,' Nathaniel said. 'He doesn't strike me as the type of fellow anyone would want mucking about in their personal business. And it wasn't as if he was ever very attentive to you in the first place, was he?'

'No, thank goodness,' Nicola said. 'I can only hope he's telling the truth when he says he shan't bother about me anymore. The way my luck's been going lately, I hardly dare believe it.'

Nathaniel, not looking at her, but at the vase of yellow roses on the table beside his end of the couch, said, 'I wouldn't say that. I think your luck's been extraordinarily good lately.'

This time the laugh Nicola let out had some humour in it – but also a good deal of disbelief.

'Me?' she cried. 'Good luck? Are you mad? I get engaged to a horrid fellow who was apparently only marrying me so his father could run a railway through my parlour' – for, since Nathaniel apparently knew the truth about Mr Pease already, there was no point in trying to hide it from *him* – 'and you say my luck's been good?'

Nathaniel removed one of the half-blown roses from the nearby vase and, breaking the bloom off neatly, examined it.

'I'd say so.' He did not take his eyes off the flower. 'After all, you found out the truth in time, didn't you?'

'Thanks to you,' Nicola said. She could not keep a little sourness from entering her voice.

He looked up then, and that hazel-eyed gaze seemed to her a good deal brighter than she'd ever noticed before.

'It would have been better for you to find out *after* you'd married him that the bloke's a cheat and a scoundrel?' Nathaniel asked, with one dark eyebrow raised questioningly.

Nicola – whether due to the question or the penetrating look, she did not know – felt herself begin to blush.

'Well,' she said uncomfortably. 'No, of course not. But—'

'It would have been better if he hadn't been trying to use you at all,' Nathaniel finished for her. 'Yes, I agree. Still, you must admit, Nicky, as far as luck goes, if you're counting good friends, and people who care for you, you're flush with it.'

And he handed, as he spoke, the half-blown rose to her.

Nicola, who had never before been given a rose – or anything, really, except for fairly merciless teasing – by Nathaniel Sheridan, took it with a gaze turned downcast, as she could not, for the life of her, think where to look. Was this the same Nat who'd used to tie her braids to chair backs when she wasn't looking? The same Nat who was forever correcting her French pronunciation? The same Nat who'd laughed so heartily at her recitation of *Lochinvar* (which she hadn't meant to be amusing)? It seemed exceedingly odd to her that that Nat and this one, handing her handkerchiefs and roses, should be one and the same.

If Nathaniel noticed her embarrassment, he did not comment on it. Instead he said lightly, 'So I suppose your heart is broken.'

Nicola, keeping her gaze on the rose, admiring the fine-veined delicacy of each leaf, the silky texture of every deeply

130

golden petal, said, 'Of course. Wouldn't yours be? Imagine even considering such a horrid thing as laying railway tracks over those lovely meadows – not to mention through Nana's herb garden and my little nursery. What kind of wicked mind would even contemplate doing something so horrid? Clearly the Grouser has never heard that "Nature never did betray the heart that loved her".'

Nathaniel winced. 'Wordsworth, again?'

Nicola looked offended. '*Tintern Abbey*,' she said, defensively.

'Appropriate, under the circumstances, I suppose,' Nathaniel said. 'But I confess I wasn't talking about the Grouser. I meant Sebastian Bartholomew.'

Nicola dropped her gaze to the rose again. 'Oh,' she said.

Had Lord Sebastian broken her heart? she wondered. She wasn't sure. What did a broken heart feel like? Certainly a good many of her hopes and dreams were dashed. But she had found, over the past few days, as she recovered from the blow she'd received, that she was perfectly capable of coming up with new hopes and dreams. Did that mean her heart – unlike her pride, which she felt had taken a near-fatal blow – had escaped unscathed? Or only that the full enormity of what had happened hadn't quite hit her yet?

'I don't know,' Nicola said thoughtfully. 'Not irreparably broken, I imagine. They are supposed to be rather resilient, and mine oughtn't be any different from anyone else's.' Then she remembered the lily maid of Astolat, who'd died of a broken heart, and added, 'I suppose I shall have to wait and see.'

Stealing a glance at Nathaniel's profile – he was staring at another vase of roses, on a nearby sideboard – Nicola saw him nod. As he did so, that familiar lock of dark hair fell forwards into his eyes. He made no move to push it away. He'd probably, Nicola thought, grown so used to it being there that he hardly noticed it anymore.

Strange. Strange that Nicola had never before looked at Nathaniel Sheridan – *really* looked at him, as she was doing now – and noticed that his face bore planes and curves every bit as finely chiselled as Lord Sebastian's. Indeed, Nathaniel was quite as handsome as the young man to whom Nicola had once referred as the God. Would Nathaniel, she wondered, have been more godlike to her if she had not known him so long, and so well? If she were to have met him at Almack's, rather than that recitation day all those years earlier, to which he'd been dragged by his parents to watch his little sister perform, would she have thought differently of him? Would she have considered him a very great catch?

The surprising answer was yes. Nathaniel Sheridan, for all his criticism and teasing of her, was an extremely good-looking, thoroughly well-groomed young man, with shoulders every bit as imposing as Lord Sebastian's, and legs just as long. If his eye colour didn't happen to match a cloudless summer sky, it was at least a very mercurial hazel that at times reminded Nicola of the stream that ran the length of the property of Beckwell Abbey, which, especially in the autumn, was a sun-dappled green quite similar in shade to Nathaniel Sheridan's eyes.

Those eyes, as Nicola was thinking these nice thoughts about them, blinked at her, and Nicola realized with another blush that Nathaniel had caught her staring at him, and was staring right back.

Good heavens, Nicola thought with some alarm as she looked quickly away. She had felt quite as if, when their gazes met, something had passed between them. Just what it was, she could not for the life of her say. But it made her feel quite shy . . . and Nicola was not a shy girl.

'How did you know, anyway?' she asked, because she was genuinely curious, but also to keep the conversation flowing, as she was beginning to feel these long pauses were dangerous . . . a girl could get to thinking any manner of unsettling things during them.

'Know what?' Nathaniel asked in a voice that was kinder than any she'd ever heard him use before.

'About Mr Pease,' Nicola said. 'And his connection to Lord Farelly.'

'Oh,' Nathaniel said in a much flatter tone, as if he'd thought she'd been referring to something else. 'That. Yes. Well, I read about it in the newspaper. The Stockton and Darlington Company, I mean. I knew Killingworth was near Beckwell Abbey, and that there was some desire to connect the colliery with the larger towns surrounding it, and . . . well, I did think that offer for the abbey came somewhat out of the blue. No offence, but Northumberland is not exactly a part of the country that people are eager to move to these days, except perhaps to find labour. It seemed unlikely to me that whoever had made the offer on the abbey wanted it for residential or farming purposes. And the article mentioned Pease had been buying up a good deal of land in the area. It was only a guess, but a reasonable one.'

'You always did have a very sound and deductive mind,' Nicola said, grudgingly admiring. 'My compliments, Mr Sheridan.'

To her surprise, Nathaniel turned toward her, and laid a hand over the one resting in her lap, still holding on to the rose he'd given her. Nicola, shocked by this unexpected contact, looked up at him speechlessly, half-prepared for him to give some sort of joking pinch to her fingers, and make a flippant remark.

Only when Nathaniel spoke, there was nothing flippant in

his tone . . . and he did not release, much less pinch, her hand.

'I hope you don't think, Nicky,' Nathaniel said, with far more seriousness than she'd ever before heard him speak with, 'that I *wanted* to be right. About Bartholomew, I mean. I hope you know I'd have given anything – *anything* – to have been wrong, if it would have meant sparing you any kind of pain.'

As this was by far the most chivalrous and . . . well, *kind* thing that Nathaniel Sheridan had ever said to her, Nicola was struck quite dumb, and could only look up at him with wide and astonished eyes. Nathaniel looked back, his own gaze steady and filled with something Nicola could not quite put a name to. It was certainly something she had never seen in his gaze before. Again, that curious current passed between them – Nicola could not have described exactly how it felt, much less what it might have been, if her life had depended upon it – and suddenly her heart . . . her poor, sorely abused heart . . . began to speed up, like the wheels of the *Catch Me Who Can* as it accelerated around the track at Euston Square.

Who knew what might have happened next had the door to the drawing room not been thrown open at that very moment, and Eleanor, followed by the jocular Sir Hugh, had not come tripping in.

'Oh, there you are,' she cried upon seeing Nicola on the couch. 'We saw that the Grouser had left, but couldn't find you anywhere. Are you all right? He wasn't beastly to you, was he?'

'Only middling,' Nicola replied with a shaky laugh. She was terribly pleased that her friend had come bursting in at just that moment. Not only had Nathaniel, upon his sister's interruption, removed his hand from Nicola's, but he'd also looked away from her, breaking the almost hypnotic hold his gaze had seemed to have on her. Nicola had a very bad feeling that if Eleanor had not happened to appear right then, she might have gone completely off her head, and done any number of ridiculous things, such as let Nathaniel Sheridan kiss her.

Which she had to admit had become an extremely tempting thought.

And her broken engagement not even a week old! How perfectly scandalous, to be thinking so soon of kissing another! And her hostess's own brother, of all people. As if she hadn't got into enough trouble doing exactly that the last time.

And yet somehow Nicola thought kissing Nathaniel Sheridan would be a very different thing from kissing the God. Because while gods were all very well and good, there was something to be said for mere mortals. Especially mere mortals who happened to have very nice, highly kissable-looking lips, such as Nathaniel Sheridan's . . .

'I say.' Sir Hugh was looking around at all the roses in the room. 'This place has taken on a bit of a funereal tone, don't you think?'

Eleanor, appalled at her fiancé's bringing up something so morbid in front of her still-mourning friend, gave him a kick on the ankle. Sir Hugh, however, did not take the hint.

'What are you kicking me for, Eleanor? All I was saying is that if I were Miss Sparks, hanging about in this mausoleum of a room would not be at all appealing. What say you to a ride in my curricle, Miss Sparks? You haven't been out-of-doors in days, I know, and I think it would be just the thing, a little wind in your hair, and sun on your cheeks.'

Nicola looked down at the rose in her lap. A few hours before, she'd have rejected Sir Hugh's invitation out of hand, as she'd have been too frightened of running into Lord Sebastian even to consider a run through the park.

Now, however, she had the strangest feeling that Lord Sebastian – the idea of Lord Sebastian, anyway, which had always been more daunting to her than the real Lord Sebastian, in any case – had lost the last of his power over her.

'Why, thank you, Sir Hugh,' Nicola said, looking up with a smile. 'I should like that very much.'

Then, with a glance at Nathaniel, she added, 'That is, if the Sheridans would join us.'

Eleanor said, 'Of course.'

But it was Nathaniel's answer for which Nicola found herself waiting with some suspense. His easy smile and 'It'd be my pleasure,' were as welcome to her as the sunshine that awaited them outside.

And really, out of all of it, *that* was the most curious thing of all.

Thirteen

A girl who had survived the ignominy of a broken engagement might reasonably spend the rest of the social season in hiding, far from the critical eyes – and tongues – of matrons who might be less than sympathetic toward her, as their own daughters had not yet received a proposal, let alone had the privilege of breaking one.

In fact, it might almost have been preferable for a young woman to wait until the following season to re-enter the social scene, in the hopes that by that time, her indiscretion might be forgotten, or at the very least put down as a youthful blunder.

But Nicola Sparks was no ordinary young woman. One might have attributed this to the fact that she had never known her mother, and so had never, except for her time at Madame Vieuxvincent's, been schooled in the appropriate course of action in such a case as this.

Or it might have been something innate within Nicola that would not allow her to shrink, as so many young women had before her, into social anonymity, following her public scandal.

Whichever the case, the fact was, Nicola passed only a week out of public scrutiny. The following Wednesday she was right back at Almack's, where her reception from the hostesses installed there was chilly, but not completely lacking in sympathy.

For it could not be forgotten that Nicola was an orphan, with only Lord Renshaw in the way of parental guidance. And of course anyone who knew Lord Renshaw – and everyone, much to their regret, did know Lord Renshaw – could have nothing but pity for his ward. Though there were a great many people who felt a good deal more sympathetic toward the rich and handsome Viscount Farnsworth than they did toward the lowly Miss Sparks, no one particularly despised Nicola for what she'd done, as the general thinking was that she was very young, and hadn't, until recently, had much in the way of adult supervision.

And so upon her arrival at Almack's the Wednesday following her breaking off her engagement, there was a minimum of nastiness toward Nicola . . . but a great, great deal of curiosity.

'But *why* did you do it?' Stella Ashton wanted to know. Nicola had barely made it out of the ladies' cloakroom before being besieged by questions pertaining to her broken engagement. 'The viscount is the handsomest man alive!'

'*I* wouldn't cast off the handsomest man alive,' declared Sophia Dunleavy. 'Not unless I discovered something very dreadful about him, such as a clubfoot, or a wife yet living.'

Stella Ashton – who Nicola was relieved to see had taken her advice about her yellow gown, and given it up for a shade of palest pink that suited her complexion a good deal better – sucked in her breath.

'Oh, say it isn't so! A wife yet living? Lord Sebastian? Wherever does he keep her? Oh, don't say Scotland!'

Nicola was forced to calm the girls' fears, explaining that Lord Sebastian had neither a clubfoot nor a secret wife in

Scotland, that she knew of. She had, she informed them, decided merely that she was too young to marry yet, and had chosen to cast the viscount back for some girl more deserving and better ready to settle down.

'And I would think,' Nicola scolded her former school-mates, 'you would be pleased I did so, as all of you might take your turn at him now.'

There was gratitude among her fellow debutantes, which was good. What Nicola most feared – that some of them might suspect the true reason behind Nicola's breaking off her engagement to the viscount – did not occur. Not a single time that evening did she hear the dreaded words, 'He was only marrying her for her property in Northumberland,' or the name of Edward Pease.

So in that way, at least, Nicola escaped some of the indignity she might otherwise have been forced to endure.

But not all of it.

Because of course if a broken engagement was not going to dissuade Nicola from attending Almack's, it most certainly wasn't going to dissuade any of the Bartholomews – who were busy maintaining an air of bewildered blame-lessness in the affair – from using their tickets, as well.

In Honoria's case, and possibly even Lady Farelly's, Nicola suspected the blamelessness might not be feigned. Honoria surely could not have known of her father and brother's wretched plans for her beloved friend's childhood home. She knew only that Nicola had, suddenly and inexplicably, broken off all relations with her family, with hardly a goodbye.

And so her reception of Nicola that evening was accordingly, and perhaps even deservedly, cool. In Honoria's eyes, Nicola had grievously injured her poor brother, a crime for which she could not soon be forgiven. Nicola could not tell the other girl the truth because, really, except for the map she'd found, she had no proof of what she suspected . . .

And the map she'd come by, of course, through less than scrupulous means.

So when Honoria, in the middle of a quadrille, cut her, Nicola pretended not to notice . . . though everyone else in the room, she was quite certain, saw it, and most likely approved. Her eyes stung at the unfairness of it all, but Nicola managed to finish the set, and even to curtsy to her partner with her usual grace and aplomb.

But that did not mean that, on the inside, her emotions weren't seething. For not only had Honoria quite cruelly snubbed her, but she had also, Nicola saw with dismay, had every last feather that Nicola and Martine had so diligently stripped away sewn back on to her gown. She looked, not to put too fine a point on it, ridiculous.

How Nicola longed to go up to her and say, 'Hate me, my lady, all you want, but for the love of God, get rid of the feathers. They don't suit you, not one bit!'

But such an outburst – at Almack's, anyway – would be unforgivable. And so Nicola bit her tongue, and tried not to look in the Lady Honoria's direction, lest the urge to pluck became too great to be borne.

Fortunately Nicola did not have to face all of this adversity alone. No, she had the protection of Lord Sheridan, who, while only a viscount, at least had a title, and a reputation for not snoring too loudly in the House of Lords, which was better than nothing. And Lady Sheridan, as well, was a well-liked and well-respected member of society. Her sheltering Nicola went a long way toward stilling many of the tongues that would ordinarily have wagged about her without stopping. If Lady Sheridan thought the girl worth sponsoring, then there must, many a matron decided, be something there worth salvaging.

And of course she also had Nathaniel, Eleanor, and Sir Hugh, all of whom had taken Nicola under their own personal care, and would not allow her to dwell upon her misfortunes. With each blow she took that evening, they soon had her rallying again . . .

At least until, across the room, she happened to spy Lord Sebastian.

Nicola had, up until that moment, avoided laying eyes upon this so-called gentleman for a week. The last time she had seen him had been when she'd told him she could not marry him.

A good many people in the assembly room seemed to know this. And so when Nicola's gaze met the viscount's, a hush fell over the people around and between them, as if everyone were waiting – and perhaps even hoping – for one of the players in the little drama erupting before them to do something interesting, such as burst into tears and run from the room, or perhaps draw a pistol and put a bullet in themselves.

When neither event transpired – Nicola chose merely to ignore the viscount, and he, after one long, inscrutable look, returned the favour – the crowds, disappointed that there was to be no bloodshed, neither emotionally nor physically, went back to what they were doing.

But Nicola, much as she tried to pretend otherwise, was affected by what had occurred far more than she cared to admit. Lord Sebastian had looked so handsome, standing there in the candlelight, his golden hair slightly tousled from dancing, and his purple evening coat, so snug-fitting, looking so fine! To think, that all of that manliness might have been hers, and hers alone! Never mind that he had turned out not –

particularly to want her. He had still chosen her, her above all others . . .

Fortunately, Eleanor noticed the warning signs, and she took Nicola by both shoulders at her earliest opportunity and gave her a slight shake.

'Jolly,' she reminded Nicola in a whisper. 'He said he loved you because you are so *jolly*.'

Which, really, was all it took to bring Nicola out of the depression into which the sight of her former fiancé had sunk her. Of course. What had she been thinking? It would never have worked out between the two of them. Lord Sebastian would have tried to convince her to sell Beckwell Abbey, for the sake of his father, and Nicola would have refused, and there would have been nothing but ill feeling in the family. She would have become the dreaded daughter-in-law, the one blamed for everything, regardless of whether or not she was the guilty party, and all because she had been so stubborn and intractable over a silly little abbey in Northumberland . . .

She wouldn't think about it. She wouldn't.

And she didn't. She was having quite a nice time sitting with Nathaniel and pointing out to him all the ways in which the other ladies present that evening might improve upon their appearance with only the slightest adjustments of their wardrobe when, from out of nowhere, the Milksop appeared.

As if Nicola's evening had not been trying enough. No, it seemed she must not only be publicly humiliated by the Bartholomews, but also plagued by her own relations.

As if he'd wished to make himself as conspicuous as possible, the Milksop had chosen that evening to wear an ensemble Nicola could only describe as *most* trying, made up of umber – no, really – sateen, with a waistcoat in a florid shade of pink. It really was most shocking. Nicola could think only that the tailor who made it had done so as a joke. If not, the man ought rightfully to be taken to a village square and immediately shot, so as to prevent him from ever again committing such a heinous crime against fashion.

'Oh, Harold,' Nicola could not help exclaiming when she saw him. 'Whatever is the matter with a black evening coat? There is nothing smarter, I think, than a man in a really well-tailored black—'

But the Milksop hadn't, apparently, any patience that night for Nicola's helpful wardrobe tips, since he interrupted her with an urgent bow.

'Cousin, may I have a word with you on a most pressing matter?' he asked, with a glance at Nathaniel. 'In *private*?'

Nathaniel, who had observed the Milksop's approach with a single raised eyebrow, said casually, 'You know, Blenkenship, it generally isn't considered at all the thing to discuss private matters at public assemblies. Why don't you call upon Miss Sparks tomorrow to discuss this pressing matter.'

It wasn't a suggestion, but a command. There could be no mistaking Nathaniel's tone.

Yet the Milksop would not be swayed. He said, his rabbity lips twitching a bit – not due to having inherited his father's sensitivity to flowers, of which there were more than a few scattered about the rooms, but to an apparent excess of emotion – 'I'm afraid that won't be possible, Mr Sheridan. I need to speak to Miss Sparks, and at once.'

Nicola sighed and, standing up, extended her hand toward her cousin.

'You may walk me up and down the room,' she said severely. 'But only once. If you cannot say all you have to say in that time, then I advise you to put the rest in a letter, as I haven't the patience tonight to listen to it . . . as I suppose you might imagine.'

This last remark referred, of course, to Nicola's current social status as a girl who'd broken off her engagement to a handsome and popular member of the assembly . . . not an enviable position to be in.

'But that's why I'm here, you see,' the Milksop hastened to explain to her in a low voice as he walked with her the length of the room, half the distance he'd been allowed during which to say his piece. 'It's about Lord Sebastian.'

Nicola, noting that a number of heads swivelled in their direction as the Milksop said this last, shot her cousin an aggravated look, and said in a hiss, 'Not so loud, please, Harold.'

The Milksop, glancing nervously about the room, lowered his voice and whispered, 'I have been trying to reach you all week. I have something very serious to discuss with you. Why have you not agreed to see me?'

'Oh, I'm sorry, Harold,' came Nicola's sarcastic reply. 'I only broke off my engagement to the man with whom I thought I'd be spending the rest of my life. I apologize for not receiving callers, but as any normal person might expect, but which apparently did not occur to you, I was prostrate with grief.'

The Milksop looked exceedingly surprised to hear this. 'You, Nicola? I don't believe it. I've never seen you prostrate before. Not even after your pony died.'

Nicola longed for her seat in the corner beside Nathaniel. There was something so very nice about Nathaniel, a fact Nicola had never, until very recently, realized. It wasn't only that he was so very attractive – although, of course, that certainly helped. But Nicola also quite enjoyed the fact that, since that day in the drawing room, they seemed to have come to a sort of unspoken understanding with one another: they were friends. While they still argued, of course – and even occasionally fought, as they had just that afternoon over the literary merits of Mr Scott's latest (Nicola thought it a masterful work, while Nathaniel put it down as pigswill for the masses) – they seemed to agree a good deal more often than they disagreed, much to Nicola's surprise. They even agreed that Sir Hugh was good for Eleanor, and that Phillip needed a good deal more discipline than he seemed to be receiving from either of his parents.

It was, on the whole, excessively strange. And excessively wonderful. And Nicola wanted to return to it just as soon as she possibly could.

'I assure you, Harold,' she said tiredly, wishing she could end this interview post-haste, 'I felt my broken engagement most keenly. Now tell me, please. What is so important that we have to discuss it here, in the middle of a ball?'

The Milksop glanced around again, though who it was he seemed so anxious to avoid overhearing them, Nicola could not imagine. The conversation seemed entirely innocuous, thus far.

'It is only that,' the Milksop said in a voice so low, Nicola had to stoop unattractively – Madame would have been shocked – to hear him properly, 'I understand that you spoke to my father the other day.'

'Yes,' Nicola said, nettled. Lord, he was such a milksop! 'What of it?'

'You told him you knew about Edward Pease, and his plans for a railway from Killingworth Colliery.'

'Yes,' Nicola said, a little surprised, it had to be admitted, that Harold should know this. 'Yes, I did.'

'You shouldn't have done that, Nicola,' the Milksop said. 'You should not have done that at all.'

145

'Should not have done what?' Nicola asked bewilderedly.

'Told Father that you knew about the connection between Edward Pease and Lord Farelly. Worse, that you knew of the plan to build the railway.'

'Why ever not?' Nicola demanded. 'It's the truth, isn't it?'

'Yes,' Harold said. 'But you oughtn't to have admitted you knew. When I told you his name – Edward Pease's name – I didn't have any idea that you suspected who he was, or what his connection to Lord Farelly might be.'

'So?' Nicola said. She greatly disliked riddles, and this was shaping up to look like the greatest riddle of all time. 'Really, Harold, what is all of this about? You are being *most* tiresome.'

It was then that the Milksop, gripping her hand very hard, dragged her toward him and said, in tones of great urgency, 'Nicola, you are in danger. Grave danger. *Danger of your life!*'

Fourteen

Nicola looked up at her cousin Harold and said, not at all impressed, 'Really, Harold. Must you be so dramatic?'

The Milksop drew a little away from her and said, looking hurt, 'I really mean it, Nicola. These men aren't joking. They mean business.'

'I'm quite sure,' Nicola said, brushing at the sleeve he'd crushed when he'd dragged her toward him. 'I suppose they are going to kill me so that your father inherits the abbey, and can sell it and collect the twelve thousand pounds himself.'

The Milksop looked appalled. 'Twelve thousand pounds? Oh, Nicola. There is a great deal more money involved than *that*. The twelve thousand was only your share. Father was going to get quite a bit more than that if he convinced you to sell.'

'Really,' Nicola said coolly. 'Well, isn't *that* nice?'

She looked about the ballroom. All around her, people were busy dancing and gossiping, flirting and fanning themselves. There wasn't a single other girl who looked as if she'd just found out her sole relations were plotting to kill her, then rob her of her birthright. *Really*, Nicola thought crossly. *This being blown about like a thistle business is* not *turning out the way I'd hoped.*

147

'Well?' Nicola turned her hostile gaze toward her cousin. 'Now that you've imparted your awful news, what do you propose I do about it?'

The Milksop looked alarmed. His piggy eyes blinked rapidly. 'Do?' he echoed stupidly. 'Well, isn't it obvious? You've got to go into hiding.'

'Hiding?' Nicola nearly burst out laughing. 'Oh, I hardly think so. I think it would make more sense to go to the magistrates, don't you?'

'Oh, you mustn't do that!' the Milksop exclaimed. 'Think of the scandal!'

'Harold.' Nicola glared at him. 'You said my life is in danger. Grave danger, you said. And you're worried about the scandal my going to the magistrates about it would cause? I suppose my murder would be more socially respectable?'

Harold looked sheepish. 'Well . . . perhaps I was a bit hasty. I wouldn't say grave danger. I think they mean only to frighten you a bit. I couldn't quite hear . . . I was listening at the keyhole, you see.'

'Then your information,' Nicola said drily, 'is surely a bit suspect, don't you think?'

'Nicola, I know what I heard. They are planning something – my father and Lord Farelly – and whatever it is, you can bet it isn't going to be good. If you have any sense at all, you'll leave London at once.'

She gave a delicate snort.

'Oh, dear,' the Milksop said. 'I thought that's what you'd say. Still, I thought I'd give it a try.' Then, brightening, he added, 'There's always a chance that they don't mean to kill you, you know. Perhaps they only want to frighten you . . . '

'How reassuring,' Nicola said. 'Well, if going to the magistrates won't help, what *am* I to do, then?'

148

The Milksop licked his lips. He appeared nervous . . . even more nervous than usual.

'Well,' he said. 'I have been thinking of a plan . . . it's a bit daring, though.'

Nicola could not help thinking that, to the Milksop, going down to the corner to buy a newspaper might seem daring. Nevertheless, she said with forced patience, 'Tell me, Harold.'

'Well,' Harold said, 'I don't suppose you are aware of the fact that I design clothing for men.'

Nicola's gaze dropped – with some misgiving – to the umber evening coat and breeches. 'No,' she said. 'Do you mean to tell me that you, Harold, designed this . . . ensemble you are currently wearing?'

The Milksop all but preened. 'Yes, indeed. Do you like it?'

Nicola murmured, 'It's quite . . . original.'

'I think so, too. But you know it seems as if here in England, people's tastes in men's wardrobe run very conservatively. My designs don't seem at all the thing. Which was why lately . . . well, Nicola, lately I've been thinking of decamping for . . . well, America.'

It was Nicola's turn to blink. She did so, astonishedly. 'America, Harold? *You?*'

The Milksop gave a shaky laugh. 'It's mad, I know. But I can't help thinking it might be the best plan. Father would . . . well, you know he would never support my going into the fashion business. But in America, you see, I could make a fresh start. And people are a good deal more accepting of new things in America.'

Nicola could not help feeling a pang of pity for residents of Boston or New York, who would soon be subjected to her cousin Harold's whimsical ideas of what men's clothing should be.

'Oh,' was all she said, however. 'How nice for you.'

It was at this point that Harold reached out and took her hand once more. On his bland, pasty-skinned face was a look of agitation.

'No, Nicola,' he said. 'You don't understand. I'm asking you to come with me to America. You know – I know you do – a good deal about dressmaking and things. I was thinking that you could help me to open a little shop. Together we could bring daring fashion to the United States . . . And you'd be safe there, you see.'

Nicola could not help feeling touched by this generous invitation. Still, she had no more desire to move to America with the Milksop than she had to allow a steam locomotive to roll through her front parlour.

'Harold, that *is* kind of you,' she said, giving his hand a squeeze, and then dropping it, as his fingers had grown quite damp in hers. 'But as I'm sure you're aware, I've never been one to run from a battle, and now is really no different.'

The Milksop looked disappointed, but not surprised. His shoulders slumped beneath the pads in his absurd evening coat, he said, 'I did think as much. But just in case you change your mind, I want you to know I've taken passage on a ship that leaves tomorrow night for Philadelphia. I've got a room at the inn across from the slip where the boat's docked . . . the White Dog. I'll be there if you need to find me.'

'I won't,' Nicola assured him, just as Nathaniel stepped up and said, in that voice she had always found insufferably teasing, but which now she knew was merely friendly, 'Nicky, the Sir Roger's coming up next. Will you have a go at it with me? You promised last week.'

Nicola had promised no such thing. Nathaniel, bless him,

was only trying to help, apparently thinking that Harold was trying to procure her hand for the next dance, not lure her to America with the information that her uncle was looking to kill her.

She explained as much when, moments later, they were dancing together.

'Kill you?' Nathaniel cried, looking very shocked indeed. 'Nicky!'

'Well, maybe not kill me,' Nicola said. 'Maybe they only intend to frighten me. Harold wasn't particularly sure. He was listening at the keyhole, you see.'

'We've got to inform the magistrates at once,' Nathaniel said, his grip on her hand very tight.

'And tell them what, Nat? That my cousin, who has always been something of an alarmist, thinks he heard his father say he intends to kill me?'

Nathaniel frowned. Even frowning, Nicola was somewhat stunned to note, Nathaniel Sheridan looked handsome.

'This is serious, Nicky,' Nathaniel said. 'I'm going to speak to my father about it. There must be something—'

Alarmed, Nicola cried, 'Oh, Nat, don't! Please don't say anything to your father. I don't want everyone in the world to know that Sebastian Bartholomew was only marrying me because his father wanted to put a railway through my family home. It's bad enough,' she added bitterly, 'that *you* know it.'

Nathaniel, though they were in the middle of a dance, stopped moving suddenly, and looked down at her with unnaturally bright eyes that, in the candlelight, seemed to glow almost gold, like a cat's.

'Nicola,' he said, in a voice much fuller than his usual tone. The deepness of his tone, coupled with the cat eyes and the fact that Nathaniel only rarely referred to her as anything but Nicky, caused her to take a quick, involuntary step backwards . . .

. . . ensuring that she would never learn what it was Nathaniel had been about to say to her, as she collided into the man who'd come up behind her.

'Miss Sparks.'

Nicola, who'd lost her balance, nearly stumbled again at the familiar voice. But Lord Sebastian, into whom she'd crashed, reached out a steady hand and, grasping her by the hand, righted her again.

'How fortunate that we should happen to meet like this,' the man whom she'd once thought a god said pleasantly enough. His blue eyes, however, fairly crackled with animosity, belying his friendly tone. 'I'd been hoping we might have a word.'

'She's got nothing to say to you, Farnsworth.' Nathaniel took hold of Nicola's free hand and tugged. 'Come along, Nicola.'

But Lord Sebastian kept a firm grip on Nicola's other hand.

'I rather think,' the viscount said, 'that Miss Sparks can decide for herself whether or not she has anything to say to me.'

Nicola had nothing to say to Lord Sebastian. But at the same time, she did not want to cause a scene at Almack's. Already too many heads were turning in her direction. It was quite bad enough that she was already known as the girl who'd broken off her engagement to the personable Lord Sebastian. She did not need to make things worse by being the cause of a brawl in the middle of the Sir Roger de Coverley.

'It will be all right,' she said to Nathaniel, gently slipping her fingers from his. 'I'll just be a moment.'

Nathaniel looked as if he would have liked to argue, but Nicola did not give him a chance to. Instead, she slipped her hand through the crook of Lord Sebastian's elbow, then said to that illustrious personage, out of the corner of her mouth, 'Make this quick, my lord. I haven't the time nor the patience for any nonsense.'

Lord Sebastian, nodding affably to the many matrons they passed – who, upon seeing the viscount together with his former fiancée, bent their heads together to whisper energetically – looked completely unaffected by her words.

'Come, come, Nicola,' he said as he waved to a maiden aunt some distance across the room. 'Did you really think you could avoid me for ever?'

'I was hoping so,' came Nicola's prompt reply.

'You wound me,' Lord Sebastian said, looking almost as if he meant it. 'You slay me to the quick. Why have you returned all my letters unopened?'

'Because I didn't care to read what you had to say in them,' Nicola informed him coldly.

If this bothered him, he did not let on. 'Why won't you see me when I come to call?'

'Because I despise you,' Nicola said.

'I don't believe you,' Lord Sebastian said. They'd reached a little antechamber, the only occupants of which, upon observing them, soon left, with raised eyebrows and knowing expressions. This allowed the viscount to behave even more foolishly than he was already, as there was no one about to observe him. He fell to one knee before Nicola, and, still gripping her hand, brought it to his lips.

'Nicola!' he cried. 'How can you be so cruel to a man whose only crime has been to love you too well?'

'Do get up,' Nicola said in some disgust. 'You look a fool.

And if you loved me too well, it's news to me. Last I heard, you thought me *jolly*, which I hardly consider an attribute likely to render a man in love. Now what's this I hear about your father plotting with my guardian to kill me?'

Lord Sebastian looked taken aback, which surprised Nicola a little.

'Kill you?' he echoed. 'He wouldn't dare. If you were to die, Nicola, my heart too would cease its beat.'

'Oh, do shut up about all that,' Nicola advised him. 'Tell me what your father plans to do about Beckwell Abbey. Because I won't sell. Not while I've a breath left in my body. You might as well tell him that.'

Lord Sebastian sighed, and, after climbing to his feet, reached down to brush the dust from the knees of his breeches.

'Nicola,' he said, in quite a different tone. It was, Nicola supposed, his real voice. Odd that she should be hearing it for the first time now, after everything between them was at an end. 'Why can't you just be a good girl and marry me? We'd have a nice enough time of it, you know.'

Nicola tapped her foot impatiently.

'Because I don't *want* to have a nice enough time of it,' she said with some asperity. 'When I marry, my lord, it will be because I feel for my husband – and he for me – a burning passion, the fires of which can never be quenched. We won't have a nice enough time. We will find heaven in one another's arms. Is that clear enough for you?'

Lord Sebastian's lower lip jutted out a little. Nicola supposed at first he was pouting, but then realized this was the expression her former fiancé wore when he was thinking.

'Passion's all very well,' he said, at length, 'but wouldn't you rather have fun? Because I can promise you, Nicola, if you marry me, that's what we'll have. We can even go away

154

from here, if you want. To Greece or something. I've heard there's all sorts of fun to be had in Greece.'

'I don't want to go to Greece, my lord,' Nicola said. 'What I want is to know what ridiculous plan your father and the Grouser are launching. Do you know? If you do, I'd appreciate your telling me. And if you don't, then I'd appreciate your not wasting any more of my time.'

Lord Sebastian made a face. Now, Nicola could tell, he really was beginning to pout.

'You really are the most troublesome creature, Nicola,' he complained. 'Any other girl would leap at the chance to marry me. I'm a most obliging fellow, you know.'

Nicola, unimpressed by this argument, said only, 'That's it. I'm leaving,' and turned to go.

'Wait,' Lord Sebastian cried.

Nicola paused beneath the archway leading back to the main assembly room, her expression inquisitive. 'Yes, my lord?'

The viscount sighed and, looking down at his slippers, grumbled, 'Why do you have to make everything so complicated?' Then, looking up, he said, 'Fine. All right. Yes, there was some talk of having you declared insane—'

'Committed?' Nicola squeaked, in true alarm.

'Right. To an institution. Then your uncle would be able to take over your business affairs—'

'He's *not* my uncle,' Nicola interrupted sharply.

'But,' Lord Sebastian continued as if she hadn't spoken, 'my father was able to talk him out of such a ridiculous scheme by pointing out that you've got enough friends – the Sheridans, and all – who would be likely to come out and swear to your sanity, that he'd never make it stick. So he abandoned that plan.'

Nicola, her face clouding over with anger, said through

gritted teeth, 'I should hope so! Mad! Me! I've never heard anything so ridiculous in my life.' Then, narrowing her eyes, she said, 'Well, go on. That can't be all. I imagine there was a secondary plan, should the first fail.'

'Oh, come, Nicola,' Lord Sebastian said with some impatience of his own. 'The whole world does not, despite what you evidently believe, revolve around you. I think your uncle's quite given up on the idea of ever getting hold of Beckwell Abbey.'

Nicola narrowed her eyes even more. 'Why don't I believe you?'

'Nicola, I swear!' Lord Sebastian looked annoyed. 'Yours isn't the only property in Northumberland they were looking at, you know. The fact that you won't sell will hardly put a halt to their plans of expanding. They'll simply lay the railway around Beckwell Abbey, instead of through it, and that will be an end to it.'

Nicola wasn't about to trust a young man who had, only a week ago, been perfectly willing to marry a girl with whom he was not in the least in love. But she had to admit, the viscount looked truthful enough. He seemed quite fed up with the conversation, which was proof enough he probably wasn't lying to prolong it.

'Nicky?'

They both looked up to see Nathaniel Sheridan standing in the archway, his back ramrod straight, and his jaw set . . . a little dangerously, Nicola thought. That muscle she'd noticed once before was drumming a steady beat there, as well.

Lord Sebastian noticed it, too. But he seemed to misinterpret it, if his next words were any indication.

'Don't worry,' the viscount said with some disgust in his tone as he brushed past Nathaniel on his way through the archway. 'She's all yours.'

Nicola felt her cheeks go crimson. *It's not like that*, she almost cried. *It's not like that at all!* She and Nathaniel were friends, and that was all.

But Nathaniel, rather than denying the implication in Lord Sebastian's tone, said nothing at all. Instead, he stepped out of the other young man's way. Then, once the viscount was gone, Nathaniel turned to Nicola and held out his hand.

'Come on,' he said. 'Let's go home.'

And suddenly – though it didn't make the slightest bit of sense – Nicola began to wish Lord Sebastian had been right . . . that she and Nathaniel *were* more than simply friends.

But that, of course, was ridiculous. Nathaniel Sheridan was nothing to her, except the elder brother of her most bosom friend. And a fairly annoying elder brother, at that, who was forever putting down her love for romantic poetry and dress patterns. She could not possibly wish that there were anything more between them . . .

Or could she?

Fifteen

Dear Nana,

I hope this letter finds you and Puddy well. Quite a lot has happened since I last wrote to you. I am very sorry to have to tell you that I was forced to break my engagement to Lord Sebastian. It turns out that he . . .

Nicola paused in her letter writing to nibble on the end of her quill. How, she wondered, was she to put this next part, exactly? She didn't want to upset Nana, but she didn't like to lie, either.

was not all that I thought he was – Nicola settled for writing – *But you mustn't fear that I am unhappy. Well, I was unhappy – desperately so – but I have since come to realize that sometimes these things happen for the better. So, while it looks like I shan't be a viscountess anymore, I am pleased to say that I am still your, and yours alone,*

Nicky.

There, she thought, as she read the letter over. That was just the right tone, too, not too sad, but not too silly, either. She would just add a few things about the Sheridans –

especially Nathaniel, who had been so kind to her lately. Not, of course, because she suspected that someday he and Nana might meet. Far from it! Nathaniel was about as likely to propose to Nicola as he was to walk on the moon, given the way the two of them bickered nearly constantly.

Stealing a glance at Eleanor's brother as he sat across the morning room, reading the newspaper, Nicola wondered how, after all the glowing things she'd written about the viscount, she could ever get Nana to believe that she suspected she had never loved Lord Sebastian in the first place. Oh, certainly she'd been infatuated with him! There was no doubt about that. But how could she ever have thought she loved him, when she had never even really known him? Why, she didn't have the first idea how Lord Sebastian liked his tea, or what his opinions were on the Decree of Fontainebleau, or whether he thought Mozart a genius or an opportunist.

She knew Nathaniel Sheridan's opinion on all three matters, as well as many, many more. Why, she knew that Nathaniel liked plays, but hated opera. That he enjoyed fishing, but disliked fish. That he could read the whole of a book in a single evening – even a very long, dull one – but could be just as happy to spend that evening instead assisting his younger brother in making a fortress out of dining room chairs and his mother's best tablecloths.

As if he sensed Nicola's gaze on him, Nathaniel lowered the paper he was reading and regarded her questioningly, that dark lock of hair falling over, as it often did, his right eye.

'Have I grown horns of a sudden, Miss Sparks?' Nathaniel asked in a dry tone.

'No,' Nicola said quickly, and ducked back over her letter,

as much to hide her flaming cheeks as to avoid having to meet his penetrating gaze.

'Horns,' said young Phillip Sheridan with a chuckle, as he played with one of the dogs. 'I should like to see *that*.'

'Nathaniel,' Lady Sheridan, bent over a letter of her own, said in a warning tone. 'Leave Nicola alone.'

'Gladly,' Eleanor's brother said as he turned a page of his paper.

Stuff and bother, Nicola thought, as she bit the end of her quill. *Now he probably thinks I'm in love with him. And I'm not. I'm* not. *Only* . . .

Well, Nathaniel Sheridan *did* look very nice in an evening coat. This could not be denied. Could she write that, she wondered, in her letter to Nana? Or was it more important to mention that Nathaniel had received a first in mathematics from Oxford? Which would impress Nana more favourably, in the event that the two of them ever did happen to meet? The evening coat, or the first in mathematics? Or should she mention neither, and write instead that the eldest Sheridan had eyes the colour of the river Tweed in autumn?

The Sheridans' butler entered the morning room with a letter on a silver salver.

'This just arrived,' Winters intoned dully, 'for Miss Sparks, madam.'

Lady Sheridan waved the butler away, being absorbed in a long letter to her sister describing why now was not the best time for a visit from her and her seven children.

Winters bowed, and presented Nicola with the salver. As Nicola did not, as a rule, receive many letters by special delivery, she was conscious of both Eleanor's as well as her brother's gazes upon her as she tore open the seal and read the following:

My dearest Miss Sparks,

I am in a fix from which only you, with your keen eye for fashion, can rescue me. I want to purchase a shawl for Eleanor, but am in a quandary over the pattern and colour. I am at Grafton House. Be an angel and help a man desperate to surprise his one and only love? I hope I need not add that your discretion is required, as the shawl is to be a surprise for our one-month anniversary. Come at once?

Beseechingly,
Sir Hugh

It was all Nicola could do not to rush at once from her chair. She had always known she liked Sir Hugh, but this . . . well, this for ever sealed for him a place in her heart. Imagine, a man so much in love that he remembered a one-month anniversary! And wished to mark the occasion with a shawl! Never mind that such a personal gift would surely be confiscated by Lady Sheridan, who, being old-fashioned, thought the only acceptable presents between men and women who were not married were flowers, chocolate and books.

And how sweet that Sir Hugh should recognize that, of all people, Nicola really was the most appropriate to appeal to when purchasing a gift of clothing. For who knew more about clothing than Nicola? No one in the whole of London.

'I hope it isn't bad news, Nicky,' Eleanor said worriedly from the chair in which she sat reading.

'You can tell by her face that it isn't,' Nathaniel said with some amusement. 'She looks like a cat that's got into the creamery.'

Casually, Nicola folded the letter, slipped it into her sleeve, and rose.

'Oh,' she said, in a tone she hoped they'd consider airy and unconcerned. 'It's from Stella Ashton. She's in fits over what to wear to the theatre tonight. She wants me to come to her house and help her decide.'

Eleanor, nodding, turned back to her book. 'Well, that's hardly surprising. After all, if it weren't for you, she'd still be wearing that dreadful yellow.'

'You aren't actually going to go, are you?' Nathaniel asked, looking astonished.

'Of course I am,' Nicola said. 'She quite needs me.'

'To help her get *dressed*?'

'Of course not,' Nicola said scornfully. 'She has a maid for that. She needs me to help her decide what to put on in the first place.'

Astonishment changing to disgust, Nathaniel put down his paper, stood up, and, with a shake of his head that seemed clearly to say, *Women*, left the room.

Nicola, thinking that Nathaniel might learn a thing from Sir Hugh, who was now her ideal of all that was manly, asked, 'May I go, Lady Sheridan?'

'Of course, my dear,' Lady Sheridan said, not looking up from her letter. 'But do be home in time for luncheon.'

'I'll be home long before luncheon,' Nicola assured her. And then she went to fetch her bonnet and gloves.

Her escape secured, Nicola was somewhat at a loss as how to proceed once she'd reached the street. For Sir Hugh had said nothing of how she was to get to Grafton House. Young ladies did not, as a general thing, go about London – even the fashionable parts – unescorted.

But there seemed to be no help for it. Sir Hugh would doubtless drive her home, but it was up to Nicola to find her own way to the shop, which fortunately wasn't far from where the Sheridans lived.

162

Still, Nicola did not think that a girl in her position – with a recently broken engagement – could very well afford to be seen walking alone along the street. Snide comments might be made by those who were already all too willing to find fault with the behaviour of a girl who would slight so estimable a personage as the Viscount Farnsworth.

And so, after having examined the contents of her reticule, and finding in it money enough to hire a hackney cab, Nicola decided to do just that.

Fortunately there was one coming her way that appeared to be empty. Indeed, as Nicola held up her hand to signal to it, the driver slowed down his horse. She was in luck.

Accepting the driver's help into the carriage, Nicola settled upon the leather seat and said crisply, 'Grafton House, please.'

'As you wish, miss,' the driver said, and he chirruped to his horse.

Nicola leaned back and thought to herself how surprised Eleanor was going to be when she received her shawl. For even though Nicola had not yet seen the shawls between which Sir Hugh was apparently trying to decide, she already knew precisely the one Eleanor was going to get: a bright yellow one of Chinese silk, decorated with blue and green peacocks. The two girls had already seen and exclaimed over it the last time they had been in the store. It was monstrously expensive, but Sir Hugh, Nicola thought, could afford it. Besides, he would want to get Eleanor the best, wouldn't he? And the peacock green would bring out the emerald in Eleanor's hazel eyes.

It was as Nicola was imagining a pleasant scenario in which Nathaniel, having observed the great joy of his sister as she opened her gift from her beau, turned to Nicola and said, 'Well, how about it, Nicky? Should we give it a go, as well?' that she realized she did not recognize her surroundings. They were not heading towards the part of London where Grafton House was located. In fact, Nicola could not even say what part of London she was in, save that it was not a part to which she had ever been before.

'I say,' Nicola said, leaning forward to speak to the driver. 'Perhaps you didn't understand. I said Grafton House. You do know where that is, don't you? Because I don't believe you're going the right way.'

To which the driver's only response was to whip his horse into a canter.

Nicola, jolted by the sudden increase in speed, fell back against the seat. *Good Lord!* What was happening? Was the man drunk? It would be just her luck to have hired a drunken cab driver.

'Sir,' Nicola cried as the unfamiliar – and not very nice-looking, for they seemed to be growing seedier with every acre – houses whizzed past. 'I think there has been some mistake. I said Grafton House. Grafton House!'

But the driver paid not the slightest heed.

Nicola, for the first time, began to feel a little afraid. Wherever was he taking her? And why? She could not help thinking about a story Martine had once told her about a man who'd lost his wife, and missed her so much that when he happened to chance upon a woman who resembled her, he kidnapped her and brought her to his home, and ordered her about as if she were his wife in truth. The girl had got away in the end, but only after suffering the indignity of having to do the entire family's laundry.

Nicola did not want to do this man's laundry – or anyone's laundry, for that matter. How positively odious!

Then, as the houses they passed grew ever more questionable, it began to occur to Nicola that the driver might have something a good deal more nefarious in mind than forcing her to do his laundry.

And so she leaned forward – difficult given the speed with which the carriage was hurtling down the narrow streets – and did the only thing she could think of, which was to jab her fingers into the driver's eyes.

Only her valiant action did not have the desired effect. For instead of howling in pain and pulling up on the reins, forcing the cab to slow down and affording Nicola a chance to escape, the driver, with a curse, reached over and pushed Nicola, by the face, unceremoniously back into her seat.

'Any more of that,' the driver snarled at her, 'and I'll bind and gag you. See if I don't!'

This was alarming information, to say the very least. Nicola lay where the driver had pushed her, her bonnet irreparably dented, and her reticule quite lost. But she gave no particular thought to these two incidentals. All she could think was, *Why, I am being kidnapped! Kidnapped, in broad daylight!*

She thought about screaming, but remembered the warning about him gagging her. The last thing that Nicola wanted was some foul-smelling article of the driver's clothing being stuffed into her mouth. She knew it would be foul-smelling because the man's hand, as it had flattened across her face and shoved her, had smelled quite bad. She highly doubted he possessed, much less carried with him, a clean handkerchief. And so undoubtedly the object that would be used to silence her would be a nasty, dirty one. Nicola would not have been able to abide anything of the sort.

Besides, Nicola thought bleakly, as the carriage thundered down the twisting, narrow road, it wasn't very likely that, even if she did get out a few screams, anyone in this neighbourhood would come rushing to her rescue. The few

165

people she happened to glimpse looked about as seedy as the houses did. She was most certainly not in Mayfair anymore, where a woman's scream would bring a Bow Street Runner, and very likely a half dozen stalwart footmen, running. More likely, in this neighbourhood a scream would bring a throng of onlookers, eager to witness the murder of a young society miss.

And if she were to jump? Make a spectacular leap from the carriage, and to safety? She would surely dash her brains upon the cobblestones below, if she managed to avoid being trampled to death beneath the hooves of the horse, or cut in half by the vehicle's wheels.

Oh! And what, Nicola could not help wondering, were her chances of being rescued? Quite small, actually, as no one had the slightest idea where she'd gone. There was a chance that Sir Hugh, when she failed to show up to meet him, would go to the Sheridans' to investigate. But who was to say, given the current circumstances, that Sir Hugh really had written that note? It could easily have been forged. Nicola was not at all familiar with the handwriting of Eleanor's fiancé. How could she be?

But if Sir Hugh had not written that note, who had?

And then, all too soon, Nicola had an answer to that question. Because the driver was hauling on the reins, bringing his animal to a halt. Nicola, half-collapsed against the bottom of the cab – which was quite grimy, having seen the bottom of a good number of shoes in the recent past – struggled to sit up, and perhaps make an escape.

But the driver seemed to know what she was thinking, and in a trice had reached into the carriage and hauled her out as roughly as if she were a sack of potatoes.

'Unhand me, sir!' Nicola cried with spirit – though it had to be admitted that her voice shook a little. 'How dare you mistreat me in this manner? I will see you imprisoned for this!'

The driver, unimpressed, dragged her by the arm into a mean, low-ceilinged building next to which he'd pulled up. Nicola had time only to glance around and see that, much to her surprise, she was by the water – seagulls sat on casks all around, while, behind them, loomed the masts of sailing ships. The tang of salt was in the air, and a rigorous breeze whipped her cheeks.

Then the driver was pushing her through a narrow door. It took Nicola's eyes a moment to adjust to the darkness of the interior after the bright sunshine outside. But when she finally could see, it was not the driver's nine children and mounds of washing that greeted her, as she'd almost come to expect.

No, it was the familiar – and not particularly welcome – face of someone she knew only too well, smiling at her from a small, bare table, at which he sat with his plump hands resting atop a silver-topped cane.

'Hello, Nicola,' said Lord Farelly.

Sixteen

'You!' Nicola burst out.

'Yes,' Lord Farelly said pleasantly. 'It is I. Thank you so much for joining us. I apologize for the ignominious manner in which you were conducted here. But you will understand, of course, that we did not think an invitation would do the trick.'

'Stubborn,' came another all-too-familiar voice. 'She was always horribly stubborn. Takes after her father in that way.'

Nicola, blinking in the dim light, turned her head towards the voice.

'Lord Renshaw,' she said, recognizing the nattily garbed figure without much surprise. 'I should have known.'

'Yes.' The Grouser scooted back his chair and stood up. 'All that money wasted on a fancy education that really does not seem to have done you a bit of good, does it? We ought just to have thrown it down the well.'

Nicola, now that her vision had at last cleared, was able to see that she stood in what appeared to be an abandoned taproom. There was a long bar to one side, over which hung a warped and not very clean mirror. A rickety-looking staircase leading to an upper floor ran along the opposite wall. Gathered at the various grimy tables along the taproom floor were a number of individuals with whom Nicola was more than a little acquainted. Lord Farelly, of course, was one, as was the Grouser. But Lord Sebastian, she soon saw, was there as well, lolling with his long legs stretched out before him, looking quite pleased with himself.

And there, at a table quite in the back of the room, sat another person Nicola knew, but had hardly expected to see in a situation such as this.

'Harold!' she cried, really feeling as if the breath had been taken right out of her. 'How *could* you?'

Harold – looking, it had to be admitted, quite miserable, though whether due to the circumstances in which he found himself or the horrid vermilion waistcoat he wore beneath a powder-blue morning coat, Nicola couldn't say – slumped in his chair, and said, 'I'm sorry, Nicola. I'm so sorry. I did try to warn you—'

'Yes.' Lord Farelly stood up, his own waistcoat, of a delicate combination of pink and green, straining a bit across his fairly prominent belly. 'And I can't say we thank you very much for that, Mr Blenkenship . . . though luckily no harm was done.'

The Milksop, looking close to tears, rose with such abruptness that his own chair fell over backward behind him with a clatter.

'Animals!' he shouted, his pale face looking round as the moon in the dismal lighting. 'That's all you are! Horrible, disgusting animals!'

'For God's sake, Harold,' the Grouser said from beneath his handkerchief, which he'd brought out and laid across his nose. 'Shut up. And be still, won't you? You're raising all sorts of dust. Whoever owns this place, Farelly, ought to be shot. Such scandalous housekeeping I've never before seen in my life. A man could choke on all this dust—'

'Where's my guinea?' the driver of Nicola's hackney cab interrupted gutturally.

'Never mind about your pay,' Lord Farelly said. 'You'll get it in good time. Now be a good lad, and make sure no one comes in.'

The driver grunted and opened the front door – letting in a bar of sunlight – then slammed it closed behind him, raising another cloud of dust, and causing the Grouser to begin coughing.

'A guinea?' Nicola, despite her fear, glared at Lord Farelly. 'That's all you had to put up for my abduction? One *guinea*?'

'I am a man,' Lord Farelly said, leaning lightly upon his decorative cane, 'who appreciates a bargain when he sees one. Surely you can't hold that against me, Miss Sparks. Thrift is generally considered a virtue, you know.'

Nicola, though she did not feel particularly brave, nevertheless snorted. Madame had always frowned upon this method of communicating one's feelings, but Nicola supposed Madame would agree that most rules of etiquette could be waived in the case of kidnapping.

'Oh, yes,' she said sarcastically. 'Your economy is truly to be applauded, my lord.'

It was at this point that Lord Sebastian, after a languorous stretch, rose and said in his lazy drawl, 'Look, can't we get this over with? I've a man to see about a horse.'

'Another one?' The Grouser lowered his handkerchief and eyed the viscount disapprovingly. 'Didn't you just buy a horse a month ago?'

The viscount shot Lord Renshaw a disgusted look. 'Can a man have too many horses?'

'As a matter of fact,' the Grouser said, 'yes, I think—'

'Enough.' Lord Farelly reached down and pulled out a spindle-backed chair. 'I believe we've all forgotten our manners. There is, after all, a lady present. Miss Sparks? Won't you sit down, my dear?'

Nicola, primly folding her hands in front of her, said, 'Thank you, no. I'd prefer to stand.'

'*Sit!*' thundered the earl in a voice so loud that more dust was loosened from the heavy oak beams overhead, and came sprinkling down upon them like snow.

Nicola hastened to do as Lord Farelly commanded, slipping on to the chair with an unsteadily hammering heart, and a sudden inkling that she might not live out the afternoon.

'That's better,' the earl said in his normal voice. He even smiled down at her . . . much the way he had smiled that day he'd taken her to ride the *Catch Me Who Can*. 'Now. Would you care for anything to drink? There's no tea, I'm sorry to say, but I could get you a glass of ale . . .'

'No, thank you,' Nicola said meekly. 'I'm quite all right.'

'Fine. Fine, then.'

And then the earl pulled out another chair, spun it around, and settled upon it, only backwards, so that his elbows rested across the chair back as he gazed down at Nicola with a kindly expression on his face.

Only this time, Nicola knew better than to trust it.

'We are, as you might have guessed, Miss Sparks, in a bit of difficulty,' Lord Farelly explained. 'You see, I am a partner in a firm called Stockton and Darlington. Do you know it?'

Nicola thought it wiser not to admit that she'd read all about the company, courtesy of his lordship's private correspondence, which she'd come across while rifling through his desk drawers.

'No, my lord,' she said, widening her eyes to appear all the more innocent.

It seemed to work. Lord Farelly said, 'No, of course

171

you've never heard of it. Well, the Stockton and Darlington Company is in the coal business. It is our goal to see that everyone in England – and, eventually, the world – has access to our product. A noble enough goal, would you not agree, my dear?'

Nicola, after a brief glance at her guardian to see if there was to be any mercy from that quarter, nodded. The Grouse was busy digging out the contents of his nostrils. There was to be no help from him, she saw at once.

'The problem,' his lordship went on, 'is that we need a better delivery system for our coal. We've used horses for years, but the problem with horses, Miss Sparks, is that they can haul only so much without getting tired . . . no matter how hard you whip them. That's why lately we've been working on a revolutionary new way of distributing our product. I believe you are familiar with this particular innovation. In fact, you've ridden on one.'

Nicola nodded, conscious that both the Grouser and Lord Sebastian, as well as his father, were staring at her. The Milksop was slumped against the bar, his head resting against his arms. He alone did not appear interested in what was happening across the room. *Thank you, Harold,* Nicola thought silently to herself. *Thank you very much, you sissified excuse for a man . . .*

'The *Catch Me Who Can*,' Nicola said carefully, because Lord Farely seemed to expect a reply of some sort.

'Correct,' the earl said, as happily as if he were a teacher with a particularly gifted pupil. 'The *Catch Me Who Can*. I took you, Miss Sparks, to ride on the *Catch Me Who Can* because I thought it might spark in you, as it had in me, an enthusiasm – a fever, you might almost say – for locomotives. For I believe that locomotives, Miss Sparks, are the way of the future. But you've heard me say so before.'

'Yes,' Nicola said, since again, some response from her seemed anticipated.

'What I'd hoped to do,' Lord Farelly went on, 'was to plant in your mind, Miss Sparks, a seed. A seed I like to call progress. Because progress, Miss Sparks, is what industry is all about. Without it, we fester, do we not? Indeed, we do. And progress, Miss Sparks, in the coal industry, is all about locomotion. With the use of locomotives, we can haul more coal to our customers than we ever could using the old-fashioned means of a horse and wagon. Do you see where I am going with this, Miss Sparks?'

Nicola nodded. She wondered if the driver was still waiting outside the door. What if she were to make a run for it? Would Lord Farelly – or his son – try to stop her? The Grouser she was certain she could outrun. But what was the point of trying if that foul-smelling cab driver was going to be there to bar the door? Perhaps there was some other way out of the building.

'It so happens that your ancestral home, Beckwell Abbey,' Lord Farelly continued, 'is smack-dab in the middle of the most direct route we were planning on using for the delivery of our coal. It was my hope that, once you became as impressed as I am, Miss Sparks, by the incredible potential afforded by these magnificent steel engines, you would recognize that some sacrifices must necessarily be made in the name of progress. Stockton and Darlington offered you what I believe was a more than generous amount for your home. It isn't, if I understand correctly, that any members of your family still live in the abbey. Still, I can see that a girl who's lost both her parents might perhaps form an attachment to even the humblest of homes, and want to cling to it as the last vestige of her family.

'But that, you see, was why I offered you a place in *my* family, Miss Sparks. To replace all you'd be losing.' Lord Farelly gestured to his son, who stood with his back against the bar, his elbows propped upon it behind him, gazing at her with those eyes she'd used to think the colour of a summer sky, but which she now equated with the hardest of ice. 'My son was very willing to marry you, and make you, in essence, my daughter. You would have had, at last, parents and a sister who love you. Moreover, you'd have had a handsome and well-off husband. You'd have been a viscountess, with all the jewels and gowns such a title suggests. All that money could buy you, Miss Sparks, I'd have gladly afforded you. And all in exchange for a house that you do not use, and which is not worth half of what we'd have gladly paid you for it.'

Here Lord Farelly's tone, which had been quite pleasant, suddenly became very unpleasant indeed.

'But what did you do?' the earl asked her, his gaze narrowing. 'How did you respond to our generosity? You broke off your engagement to my son with barely an explanation, and left our home with hardly a word of thanks!' He stabbed an index finger at her. 'You very selfishly refused to see any of us. And, worst of all, you still stubbornly clung to the idea that you are not going to sell the abbey.'

He lowered his hand and said, in a voice that was lower in volume, but no less menacing, 'And that, Miss Sparks, was a very grave mistake. Because the fact is, none of us can afford to stand in the way of progress. To do so is a betrayal. Not a betrayal of friendship, or of trust. But a betrayal of our country. Of England. Because if any of us decide to stand in the way of progress, what we are really doing is holding England back, keeping her from becoming all that she could be. And you, as a loyal citizen, would never want to do that, would you, Miss Sparks?'

Nicola, after some consideration, shook her head. Not to do so, she felt, would be unwise at this juncture. And she was gratified to see that she'd guessed rightly. Lord Farelly seemed very glad to see her head shake. He even smiled, reminding Nicola of all the many jolly conversations she'd had with him back when she'd stayed at the Bartholomews'.

Except crocodiles, Nicola reminded herself, were said to smile, as well . . . right before striking their prey.

'That's more like it,' Lord Farelly said, still smiling broadly. 'You see, Norbert? I told you she could be reasonable. You simply hadn't put the matter in as clear a light as I have. Now, Miss Sparks, perhaps we can repair this little misunderstanding, and all go about our separate ways and forget any of this unpleasantness ever happened.' His lordship reached into his waistcoat pocket and drew out a sheaf of papers. 'I just need you to sign a few things, and—'

Nicola was willing to be obliging . . . but only to a point.

'No,' she said in the smallest voice imaginable.

Lord Farelly, the papers still in his hand, glanced up briefly. 'I beg your pardon?' he said, as if he had not heard her correctly.

'I said . . . ' Nicola's throat had gone dry. She wished she hadn't turned down the earl's offer of a glass of ale. Nevertheless, she swallowed and said in the same small voice, 'No. I won't sell. And . . . ' she added, knowing it was only going to get her in trouble, but unable to help herself, 'you can't make me.'

Lord Farelly stared at her, for all the world as if she were a rock or some other inanimate object that had suddenly begun to speak. The Grouser, across the room, groaned and lifted his gaze, in evident supplication, to the ceiling. Even Lord Sebastian sucked in his breath and shook his head, while, farther down the bar, the Milksop let out a whimper, and hid his head deeper in his arms.

Lord Farelly blinked. 'What . . . did . . . you . . . say?' he asked slowly.

Nicola, though she was frightened witless, felt angrier than she did scared. Angry enough to snap, 'You heard me. I said no. I'll never sell Beckwell Abbey. But I'll tell you, if I were to sell it, the last person on earth I'd let buy it is you, Lord Farelly. Imagine, suggesting my not selling it is unpatriotic! I'll tell you what's unpatriotic: Bullying a young, defenceless orphan. That's what's unpatriotic. Why, men like you ought to be locked up!'

Lord Farelly's reaction to these words was swift and terrible. He was on his feet in a second, knocking the chair from his way as he took a single step toward Nicola, his right arm raised . . .

The Grouser moaned and hid his eyes. The Milksop had never even lifted his head, so he did not know what was happening. But Lord Sebastian, still leaning against the bar, grinned and said, 'You've done it now, Nick.'

Nicola did not flinch. She looked up into Lord Farelly's face, mottled red with rage, and said, 'Go ahead and hit me. It's exactly the kind of behaviour I'd expect from a coward like you.'

Truth be told, Nicola did not feel half so brave as she was pretending. Her heart was in her throat, and she was quite certain that, should she ever again be allowed to stand, her knees would not support her.

Nevertheless, she kept her chin thrust forward and her brows lowered over her eyes. This was, she felt, the appropriate response to a bully. For that was all the Earl of Farelly was: a great, mean bully.

Something in Nicola's attitude must have reached the tiny

part of Lord Farelly's brain that was still capable of civilized behaviour. Because, slowly – too slowly, for Nicola's peace of mind – he lowered his arm . . . though he never took his glittering gaze from her face.

'Locked up, eh?' he echoed, breaking the thick silence that had fallen across the room.

Nicola held her chin higher still. So, she imagined, had Lady Jane Grey, going to meet the chopping block, held her own chin . . . right before she helpfully removed her neckerchief, so her executioner would not miss his mark. Nicola, however, had no intention of being anywhere near as accommodating.

'That,' Nicola said rudely, 'is precisely what I hope they do to you.'

Barely was the last word out of her mouth before Lord Farelly, with another thunderous cry, swooped down and hauled her bodily from her chair.

'Then let's see how you like it,' he bellowed, propelling Nicola by one arm toward the staircase at the far end of the room. 'Go on! Upstairs with you. If you think locking someone up is so effective, let's see if it works. Perhaps a little time for some quiet reflection will cause you to see the error of *your* ways, Miss Sparks!'

And, with a great shove, Lord Farelly forced Nicola up the stairs and into a tiny room on the building's first floor, into which he thrust her, and then, with a slam, closed the door behind her. The last sound Nicola heard for some time was the scrape of the key turning in the lock.

And then she was alone.

Seventeen

'"Oh, young Lochinvar is come out of the West, through all the wide Border his steed was the best."'

Nicola, lying on her narrow and extremely uncomfortable pallet, stared up at the sloping beams above her head. It was difficult to see them in the waning light. There was only, after all, one small window to begin with, and that had been somewhat crudely boarded up.

Still, she attempted to make out the shapes of the beams against the dark wood ceiling.

'"So faithful in love, and so dauntless in war, there never was a knight like the young Lochinvar."'

Nicola's voice, in the stillness of the room, sounded curiously muffled. Perhaps that was because she had, for some time before that, been crying. She was hoarse from it, and from screaming, the sides of her fists raw from where she had beaten them against the locked door, her boot toes scuffed from her kicking them against the unyielding panel of wood. She was, she was beginning to realize, well and truly trapped.

Still, though they could lock up her body, they would never get, she'd decided, her mind. And so she strove to keep it flexible by demanding from it all the poetry that she knew.

"'For a laggard in love, and a dastard in war, was to wed the fair Ellen of brave Lochinvar"'

That was precisely who Nicola was. Fair Ellen, locked in this odious tower against her will.

But where, Nicola wondered, was her Lochinvar?

Nowhere. For Nicola had no Lochinvar. In the first place, she was not even sure anyone yet realized she was missing. And in the second, so what if she were? It wasn't as if anyone would have any clue where to begin looking. No, Nicola had seen to that with her own stupidity. Imagine, believing that silly note! Why, she ought to have known a gentleman like Sir Hugh would never purchase a shawl for his lady love. Not when he knew how much the purchase might upset his future mother-in-law.

No. Nicola was a fool, and of the first order. And look where it had got her: locked in a cell, with no chance of rescue from Lochinvar – or anyone, for that matter.

She would rot here, she was quite certain. Rot until she was nothing more than a steaming pile of bones.

And then, without warning, the key scraped once more in the lock. Nicola lifted her head from her pallet, but as the door opened, her eyes were dazzled by a sudden burst of light. She threw up a hand to shield them, but it was only, she soon discovered, the light from a candle flame. It had grown so dark in her cell that her eyes had become quite used to it.

'Well, Nicola,' said the voice not of her rescuer, but of one of her tormentors. Her guardian, to be exact. 'Quite a little dilemma you find yourself in the middle of, eh?'

Nicola, who was not in the mood to speak to the Grouser, rolled over on her pallet and stared steadily at the closest wall instead.

'Oh, not speaking to me, are we?' The Grouser did not

sound bothered by this in the least. 'Well, that's understand-able, I suppose. Still, surely by now you've had time to realize that his lordship and I . . . well, we mean business, Nicola. It truly is of no inconvenience to us to keep you locked in here for ever. You really might consider being a good girl, and giving us what we want. It will spare you a great deal of suffering in the end.'

'I won't,' Nicola said through gritted teeth, and in the direction of the wall, 'sell.'

'Ah.' The Grouser sounded a bit sad. 'I was afraid you were going to say that. I told Farelly you'd not been in here long enough. He is not used to, as I am, your bullheaded-ness. He seemed to think a few hours was all it would take. But no. He is accustomed, you see, to his own daughter, who is of course a model of femininity. Quite unlike you, Nicola, whom I am beginning to think quite unnatural. I told him it would take far more than mere imprisonment to get through to a stubborn miss like you. I am very much afraid we will have to resort to Lord Farelly's other plan.'

Nicola, hearing this, rolled over and sat up so swiftly, she came close to striking her head on one of the very roof beams she'd been staring at just moments before, so low did the ceiling slope above the bed.

'I knew it,' she cried with flashing eyes. 'I knew you intended to kill me, you murderous swine. Well, go ahead, and be swift about it, so that my soul might commence to plaguing you and drive you directly to your own grave, through madness.'

The Grouser looked a good deal taken aback by this. He stood with the candle in one hand, and his handkerchief with the other, the door wide open behind him. Still, Nicola feared that, even if she were to rush him and successfully get past, she would only encounter the cab driver belowstairs, who would turn her around and force her right back up them again.

'Kill you?' Lord Renshaw shook his head distastefully. 'Good Lord. You always were a most fanciful child. No one intends to kill you, Nicola. Except, of course, in the case of self-defence, as I swear, I sometimes fear for my own life where you are concerned, you are so brash at times. No, that is not the plan I refer to . . . though I cannot but admit that all of our lives would be a good deal simpler were you no longer in them.'

'What is it, then?' Nicola barked. 'Torture? Do you plan on sticking hot needles beneath my fingernails until I agree to sell?'

When the Grouser only blinked some more and looked confused, she went on passionately, 'Or starvation? You plan on slowly robbing me of my will by denying me food and water? Well, sorry to disappoint you, but it won't work. I will never give up the abbey. Never!'

The Grouser, frowning, said, 'You read entirely too much, my dear. No one will be sticking needles anywhere. Good Lord, how revoltingly imaginative the young can be. And as for starvation, that is entirely your prerogative, of course. But as I did go to the trouble of securing a meal for you, I would be insulted were you not even to sample it. It isn't much, I know, but . . . '

Then, going to the door, the Grouser took a tray from the hackney cab driver – if he even *was* a hackney cab driver, which Nicola was beginning rather to doubt, who was lurking about in the dark hallway. More likely he was a hired henchman of Lord Farelly's.

' . . . it should, at least, be edible.'

And the Grouser left upon a low, rickety table in one corner of the attic room a tray, on which rested a loaf of bread, some cheese, and a pitcher filled with what Nicola presumed was ale.

'There,' Lord Renshaw said with some satisfaction. 'That should do admirably for the moment. And now, as I mentioned before, I had better go and let Lord Farelly know that you remain, er, committed to your cause. He will, I believe, have some business to attend to, given the circumstances.'

And then, leaving the candle so that Nicola had some light with which to see her food, the Grouser withdrew, taking the driver with him.

Alone again in her cell, Nicola reviewed her options. There weren't many. She could, it appeared, eat her supper. Or she could save it to hurl at the head of the next person who came through the door.

On the whole, Nicola thought more of the first option, as she was both hungry and thirsty. And who knew how long it would be before someone again turned that key?

And so Nicola broke off a piece of the bread, and, finding it not too entirely stale, laid across it a piece of the cheese, and ate both. They were, as the Grouser had assured her, not much, but highly edible. She washed this frugal meal down with a few swallows of ale, which was most notable for its not being too bad.

Then, when she had eaten until she was full, she lay back down upon her cot and resumed staring at the shadows the dancing candle flame made upon the ceiling.

'"Heap on more wood,"' Nicola said, to the oak beams. '"The wind is chill. But let it whistle as it will."'

Her voice, now that it had known some succour in the form of liquid refreshment, was stronger. She was quoting with some energy, '"And dar'st thou, then, to beard the lion in his den,"' when the key again turned in the lock, and this time not the Grouser, but his son, slipped into Nicola's prison cell.

She sat up at once to whisper, 'Harold, are you here to rescue me?'

Harold, though he laid a finger to his lips, said, 'No, no. I've only come to see how you fare.'

Disappointed, Nicola lay back down and said, moodily, 'If you aren't here to set me free, then I have nothing to say to you.'

'Nicola.' The Milksop lifted an unsteady chair from a far corner of the little room, placed it by Nicola's cot, then sat upon it. 'Please don't be that way. You know if I could, I would help you in a moment.'

'Do I know that, Harold?' Nicola asked him. 'No, I don't think I do. I think that you, Harold, are incapable of thinking about anyone but yourself.'

The Milksop looked almost as hurt as he had the time she had put a grass snake down his trousers.

'Now, Nicola, that simply isn't true. If it were, would I be here? Not on your life. But you must know, escape is impossible. That horrid Grant is downstairs, quite watching the door.'

'Grant?' Nicola asked. Then she sank back against her hard pallet. 'Oh, I suppose you mean the driver.'

'Right. He's a great, strong brute, Nicola. Even if I did manage to sneak you from here, there's only one way out, and he's blocking it.'

'And I don't suppose,' Nicola said, 'that it would have occurred to you to have gone for help.'

The Milksop looked appalled. 'Help? Oh, Nicola. Then everyone would find out . . . '

'Find out what?'

'Well,' the Milksop said shamefacedly, 'what a monster my father is.'

'Harold,' Nicola said. 'What difference does it make? I thought you were running away to America.'

'I am,' Harold said. 'But a thing like that . . . well, it can follow a man, even across an ocean. I honestly can't afford the talk it would cause, Nicola. You understand, don't you?'

Nicola laughed, though bitterly. 'Oh, certainly, Harold. I understand that an up-and-coming designer of men's fashions can't afford to have a lot of loose talk about his father being a murderer of innocent young girls . . . '

'Oh, but he doesn't intend to murder you, Nicola,' Harold said lightly. 'They don't intend to harm you at all. They only mean to make you marry Lord Sebastian—'

'*What?*' Nicola cried, sitting up fast, and again narrowly missing smacking her head against the roof beams.

'That's right,' Harold said, looking a little taken aback. 'Lord Farelly, it turns out, secured a special licence some time ago. He's gone out to fetch a parson. They mean to make you marry the viscount tonight, so that he can sell the abbey, since you won't do it.'

'They can't do that!' Nicola swung her legs from the bed and stood up.

'I'm afraid they can,' Harold said apologetically. 'Even though you're underage, my father is your guardian, so all he has to do is give permission for the match. And since, as man and wife, what's yours is his, Lord Sebastian would be well within his rights to sell the abbey, no matter what you say.'

'That's . . . that's . . . that's *preposterous*!' Nicola shouted, giving the rickety table that held the remnants of her evening meal a kick, so that the leftover ale sloshed over the side of the pitcher that held it. 'I won't stand for it, do you hear, Harold? And I won't say "I do." I can promise you that!'

Harold looked concerned. His dark eyebrows constricted in his bland, moonlike face.

'I don't think this particular parson will care,' the Milksop said. 'He's a close friend of Father's. The two of them were at school together.'

Nicola let out a strangled scream, and then, much to the alarm of the Milksop, bent down and seized him by the collar of his coat.

'Now you listen to me, Harold,' Nicola said in a hiss, her face just inches from his. 'And listen well. You are going to go downstairs, and you are going to make up some kind of excuse – I don't care what – and then you are going to leave here. And then you are going to go to Mayfair, where you are going to tell Lord Sheridan precisely what's happening here. Do you understand me?'

The Milksop's pouting lips fell open. 'B-but, Nicola—'

'No, Harold,' Nicola whispered hoarsely. 'Not this time. You are not going to weasel your way out of this one. For once in your life, you are going to prove that you have a backbone. You are going to do the right thing. Otherwise, Harold, if I live through this, I will go to the press, and I will tell them that you were the mastermind behind the entire plot, do you hear me? How do you think your future clients in America are going to like hearing *that*?'

The Milksop's jowls began to quiver. He looked to Nicola to be on the verge of tears. Indeed, she could see the drops of moisture already gathering at the corners of his piglike eyes.

'All . . . all right, Nicola,' he stammered finally. 'I'll . . . I'll do it. Only don't . . . don't go to the press. Please. I beg you.'

Nicola released his coat collar and took a step backwards. 'I won't,' she said. 'If you do the right thing.'

'I will,' Harold said, climbing shakily to his feet. 'I swear I will, Nicky.'

And then, still fighting back tears, the Milksop staggered through the door, closing it softly behind him, and then, almost sheepishly, turning the key in the lock.

Nicola, hearing this, only stood and stared at the solid portal, her heart drumming an uneven, too-rapid beat within her chest. Because, for the first time, she was frightened. Not for herself. She'd been frightened for herself all day.

But now she found herself fearing not for her own life, but for the lives of the people she loved. For it seemed to her that at last Lord Farelly had found a way to win, and that meant the end for Nana and Puddy, and the tenant farmers, and all the people who depended upon Beckwell Abbey for their livelihoods.

Unless . . . unless Harold could somehow find a way to be a man. It was, she knew, a very slim chance. Still, it was a chance.

And in any case, Nicola herself was as prepared as she could ever be, she supposed, for battle.

'"Charge, Chester, charge,"' she whispered fiercely to the closed door. '"On, Stanley, on! Were the last words of Marmion."'

Eighteen

'Ah,' said Lord Sebastian, after he'd flung open the door to Nicola's prison and found her seated meekly upon her cot. Leaning in the doorway with his arms folded across his chest, he regarded her with no small amount of interest. 'The blushing bride.'

'It's bad luck,' Nicola informed him, 'for the groom to see the bride before the ceremony.'

'Bad luck.' Lord Sebastian chuckled, then sauntered casually into the room, having to duck a bit, because he was so tall, in order to avoid the beams overhead. 'It would seem so. For the both of us. It isn't exactly my dream, you know, to marry a girl who claims to despise the very ground on which I walk.'

'Well, it isn't exactly my dream,' Nicola pointed out, 'to marry a man who seems to think everyone should worship the ground on which he walks.'

'Touché,' the viscount said with a wry smile. He really was, Nicola couldn't help reflecting, very handsome.

Too bad he was so well aware of the fact.

'What do you want, my lord?' Nicola inquired from the bed. 'Has your father returned with the minister?'

'Not yet,' Lord Sebastian said amiably enough as he bent to break a piece of bread off the loaf on the table. 'I just thought I'd come up here and get a few things straight before, you know, the nuptials actually take place.'

'Really,' Nicola said without enthusiasm. 'How thoughtful of you.'

'You probably won't think so' – Lord Sebastian popped the piece of bread into his mouth. He chewed, swallowed, and then commenced to licking his fingers – 'when you hear what I've come to say. But here goes, anyway. Number one. I am no more excited about this than you, Miss Sparks, so you can set aside any fears that you might have that I have any intention of the two of us ever living as man and wife.'

'Oh?' Nicola said politely.

'Right. I intend to keep rooms at my club. You can reside with Mama and Honoria. I'm certain they will enjoy your company a good deal more than I ever could. All that incessant chatter about poetry!' He rolled his expressive blue eyes. 'I swear, there were times I thought I might go mad if I had to listen to it any more.'

'How illuminating,' Nicola said. 'Pray go on.'

'Number two,' the viscount continued, 'you will afford me the respect and courtesy that a wife should. As your husband, I shall expect my word to be law. You will behave as I instruct you, or you will find yourself locked right back in this room quicker than you can say Jack Robinson.'

'I see,' Nicola said.

'Number three,' Lord Sebastian said, ticking off each point on his fingers. 'You will, at all times, maintain a neat and appealing appearance. None of this trying to put me off by failing to clean your teeth or wash your hair. You will remember that you are a viscountess, and conduct yourself accordingly.'

'Indeed,' Nicola said.

'Four, you will not squander my money on gewgaws. You will, of course, be afforded an allowance, but you will be expected to keep your spending within a certain budget. Are you getting all this?'

Nicola nodded reverently. 'Yes, my lord.'

Pleased at the apparent change in her attitude, he went on. 'Number five. As far as providing me with an heir you will, of course, produce a son within the year.'

'Won't that be difficult,' Nicola asked sweetly, 'if we are maintaining separate residences?'

Lord Sebastian frowned. He had evidently not thought of this.

'We will have to have intimate contact with one another occasionally,' he admitted. 'Perhaps I will stay at home from my club on Saturday and Sunday evenings.'

'That sounds a very sensible plan,' Nicola said.

Lord Sebastian smiled at finding her so complaisant, and reached for a piece of cheese.

'I can foresee,' he said, chewing, 'that so long as you can remember the items I just described, and keep the chatter to a minimum, you and I shall get on capitally, Miss Sparks. For you are, for all your faults of character, quite fetching to look at. Really, I never considered being married to you at all a burden. I rather looked forward to it, in fact. A man likes to have some stability in his life, you see, and having a pretty wife to come home to at the end of a long day at the races or the card table must always be considered a boon. If you can just keep that tongue of yours in check, Nicola, I would say that we have a very good chance at finding marital bliss. Don't you think?'

Nicola, from her pallet, said meekly, 'If you say so, my lord.'

'Well.' Lord Sebastian regarded her with some surprise.

'I do say so. I declare, Nicola, but you're being awfully obliging. I'd have had Father lock you up long ago if I'd known it was going to have this kind of effect on you. I must say, I really think we have a shot at a decent marriage, don't you?'

Nicola smiled at him. 'As good a shot as anyone, I'm sure, my lord.'

Looking immensely satisfied, Lord Sebastian said, 'Well, I'm excessively glad we had this little chat.' Then, with a glance at the table, he said, 'I thought I saw them bring up a pitcher of ale. What happened to it?'

Nicola, from the bed, asked, 'Oh, would you like a little ale, my lord?'

'Indeed,' Lord Sebastian said. 'That cheese has made me parched.'

'Well, then,' Nicola said, climbing to her feet. 'By all means, my lord, let me serve you, as a good wife should.'

And with that, Nicola swung back her arm, and, with all the force she could muster, brought the pitcher she'd been holding down upon Lord Sebastian's golden head.

The clay vessel exploded, sending pottery shards and ale flying everywhere. Nicola didn't care. She hardly noticed, in fact. She had eyes only for Lord Sebastian who, not seeming to know what had hit him, stood for a moment looking dazed, ale dripping down from his blond curls and on to the fine stitching of his silver waistcoat.

'Hark,' Nicola said. 'Do you hear wedding bells, my lord?'

Lord Sebastian nodded dumbly. Then his eyes rolled slowly back into his head, and he slumped heavily to the floor. Nicola stepped neatly out of the way, lest she inadvertently offer up a cushion for his fall, something she in no way wished to do.

Once Lord Sebastian was stretched, unconscious, upon

the floor, Nicola returned to what she'd been doing before he had so rudely interrupted her.

And that was kicking out the wooden planks that someone had fastened across the tiny window at the far end of her cell.

She heard, from downstairs, the Grouser call, 'Lord Sebastian? Lord Sebastian, is everything all right up there?' He had undoubtedly heard the thump that had been the viscount's head hitting the floor. 'Lord Sebastian, your father's here with the parson. Would you be so kind as to bring the girl down, so that we might begin the ceremony?'

Nicola, with renewed fervour, thrust her foot through the last of the boards barring her path to freedom. Being very old and weather-beaten, they crumbled obligingly.

'Just a moment,' she called, to forestall anyone coming up to look for her. 'I just want to . . . to comb my hair!'

And then, as the cool sea air hit her face, Nicola thrust her head and shoulders through the window . . .

. . . and found herself looking out of a dormer on to a rooftop a good twenty feet in the air. All around her lay shingles and smokestacks reaching up toward the starry night sky. Below her, she could see the street, narrow and all but empty this time of the evening. Not one street away lay the docks, great sailing ships standing tall and proud in their slips, their masts rising high above the rooftops like poplars in the twilit sky.

For the first time all day, Nicola began to see a glimmer of hope for her future.

'See here!' Nicola heard the Grouser shout from behind her. *Too* close behind her. He was in her cell! 'Where do you think you're going? And what . . . My God! What have you done to the viscount?'

There was no more time to sit and admire the view.

Nicola had to move, and move fast. It was a tight squeeze when it came to her hips, but she finally managed to wriggle almost all the way through the window.

Almost all the way because, even as her knees were scraping against the rough wooden shingles, one of her ankles was seized from behind, and held in a grip of iron. For such a spindly thing, Lord Renshaw was surprisingly strong.

'Come back here!' The Grouser called, tugging for all he was worth on her foot. 'Come back!'

But Nicola had already had too strong a taste of freedom to allow it to slip away from her now. Twisting like a cat, she managed, with a few well-placed kicks, to prise her foot at last from her guardian's hands . . . although she came away minus one of her shoes.

'You . . . !' The Grouser called, waving the slipper at her through the window as she limped away across the shingles – no easy feat, since many of them were rotten, and had a tendency to slide out from beneath her, skid down the sloping roof, and then fall with a clatter to the street below. 'Come back here, you ungrateful chit!'

But Nicola, having made her way across the treacherous territory, nearly losing her balance several times thanks to loose shingles, finally made it to a brick chimney some yards away. She flung both arms around it, then turned, panting, to regard Lord Renshaw in the purple gloaming.

'I won't come back,' she informed him breathlessly. 'And you can't make me.'

'Oh, can't I?' Lord Renshaw shook his head. 'You can't stay out there forever, you know, Nicola. Eventually it will start to rain . . . or you'll slip. You'll fall to your death, you stupid girl.'

'I don't care,' Nicola retorted. 'So long as I don't have to marry the viscount.'

'Marry him!' The Grouser cried. 'Why, you'll be lucky if you haven't killed him. Murder's a hanging offense, you know!'

Nicola reflected that, were she to hang for the viscount's murder, Lord Renshaw would get Beckwell Abbey after all, in the end. But she knew Lord Sebastian wasn't dead. He'd been breathing quite evenly when last she'd looked. Besides, it had only been a clay pitcher. He'd wake with a headache, surely, but no shards in his skull. She doubted she'd even managed to scar his beautiful, manly head.

'You come back here right now, Nicola Sparks,' the Grouser cried, having to break off every few words in order to cough into his handkerchief, as there was apparently a good deal his tender throat found objectionable in the evening air. 'You come back here this minute, before you slip and crack your head open.'

'No,' Nicola said, and she sat down upon the slippery shingles – made all the more hazardous by her having on only a single shoe – and, trying not to notice how thoroughly she was shaking – though not because it was cold, as the temperature was quite mild – refused to budge. Indeed, she was not certain she could have moved if she'd wanted to. It was terrifying to be that high in the air, without even remotely firm footing. She was much better off, she decided, where she was.

Lord Renshaw's voice was soon joined by another. Lord Farelly had come upstairs, and now peered out at her angrily.

'I'll have you clapped in irons for this,' he shouted, being entirely too stout to follow her out the window, though, judging from the red rage in his face, he wanted to, very badly. 'If you've killed my boy, you harpy—'

'He isn't dead,' Nicola said disgustedly.

'I shall send Grant out after you,' the earl bellowed. 'See if I won't.'

But the driver, Nicola knew, could no sooner fit through the window than Lord Farelly. The only one who might have been able to squeeze through the narrow opening was the Grouser. She could hear the men arguing inside her little attic room, as the earl tried to convince her guardian to risk it.

'I will not!' she heard the Grouser cry. 'Why, you saw what she did to your son! Do you think she'd hesitate to push me off that roof the first chance she got?'

And then, along the narrow, cobblestoned streets below, Nicola heard the clatter of horses' hooves. Someone, she realized, was coming.

And not just one person, either, but quite a few of them.

Craning her neck, Nicola tried to peer around the chimney against which she leaned. It was dark in the street – the sun had set behind the houses on the western side of it – but Nicola guessed there were at least a half dozen men approaching. They might, of course, be men with business down at the docks. Or they might be reinforcements fetched by the Milksop . . .

But no, what were the chances of that? The Milksop surely hadn't made it to Mayfair. If he'd managed to escape at all – and Nicola could only suppose he had, as she had not heard his voice joining in the cacophony inside her attic cell – he had surely run off to the ship that was to take him to America. Why should he trouble himself about a girl who'd refused, so rudely, to marry him?

And then the horsemen on the street below thundered into view. Nicola had been right – there *were* six of them – and four of them wore coats of the Bow Street Runners!

'Help!' Nicola shrieked, as, clinging to the chimney beside

her, she scrambled to her feet on the treacherously sloping roof. 'Up here!'

She saw the riders – she could not make out their faces – pull their mounts to a halt. But at the same time, she also heard a noise from behind her. Spinning around, she was horrified to see the cab driver – Grant – clambering his way over the peak in the roof. He had apparently found some other, much larger window on the opposite side of the house through which to climb.

And now he was lumbering at her with an expression of determination on his face, apparently not aware that, below, the cavalry had arrived.

'Don't worry, milord,' Grant called to Lord Farelly. 'I got 'er. I'll have 'er down in a wink.' Then, to Nicola he said, his arms spread wide to catch her if she chose to flee, 'Come 'ere, missy. I won't hurt you now.'

Nicola did not, of course, believe him. She kept her back to the chimney, but scooted as far from him as she possibly could without loosing her handhold.

'Keep away,' Nicola warned him, as beneath his weight she heard the rooftop groaning. 'The shingles are loose here. You'll fall.'

But the driver still made his way toward her, pieces of shingle splintering beneath his feet and sliding down the far side of the roof, to tumble off and then land, with a crack, in the washyard behind the house.

'Just a little farther,' Grant said, as he inched ever closer to her. He seemed insensible of the danger he was thrusting them both into. 'Give me your hand, missy.'

'I won't,' Nicola declared, clinging fast and hard to the chimney.

'Gimme me your bleedin' hand,' the driver commanded. He was only a foot away now. Nicola could smell plainly that he'd spent the long hours she'd been locked up in the attic sampling the taproom's many kegs of ale. His eyes were red and bleary-looking, and there was a coarse growth of razor stubble sprouting from his neck and cheeks. 'I'll help you down.'

'Help me down?' Nicola let out a bitter laugh. 'Pull me down, and to my death, more likely.'

A split second later, she greatly regretted her flippant words. Because suddenly it was as if they'd become a prophecy. The driver, just as he came over the crest in the roof and stepped to Nicola's side, widened his eyes in alarm as, beneath his feet, a great section of shingles gave way. He began to slide – slowly, so slowly, at first – down the incline. He attempted to stop his descent by reaching out and seizing the first thing his fingers closed over.

Which happened to be the skirt of Nicola's dress.

She was not strong enough to hold for both of them. She could feel her fingers slowly losing their grip on the bricks to which she'd been clinging until the driver's added weight made it impossible for her to hold on any longer. Suddenly she too lost her footing . . .

And then they were both sliding down the roof, like competitors in some kind of race, until suddenly there was no more roof, and Nicola found herself careering through the air, convinced that this, at last, was the end.

Nineteen

At least until she landed, which she did with both eyes tightly closed, having no desire to witness her own death.

Except that, after collapsing with some force against something hard – but not quite as hard as cobblestones – and, in places, strangely furry, Nicola was surprised to find that, when once again she could catch her breath, she was still capable of breathing. Surely, if she were dead, this would not be possible.

Opening one eye – she was quite fearful of seeing, if not her own blood, then the cab driver's – Nicola saw not her own mangled limbs, or anyone else's, for that matter. Instead she saw an ear.

A man's ear, half-hidden in a head of dark brown hair.

Opening her other eye, Nicola was relieved to see that the head to which the ear belonged was attached to a neck, and that the neck was attached to a pair of broad shoulders coated in blue wool. Furthermore, she was able to see that the man to whom both the shoulders and the ear belonged was sitting astride a horse.

And that she, Nicola, had apparently fallen off the roof, and into the broad-shouldered man's arms.

And that the broad shouldered man was saying something to her – her name – and that, even more oddly, she recognized him. Recognized him, and, she realized in that moment, loved him.

'Nat!' she cried, and threw both her arms – mercifully unscathed by her fall, thanks to him – around his neck. 'Oh, Nat!'

'Nicky, are you all right?' Now that fear was no longer causing her blood to pound so fiercely inside her head, Nicola found that she could hear him just fine. And what she heard – the relief in his voice – was a very welcome sound indeed. 'My God, did they hurt you?'

'No, I'm fine,' Nicola assured him, clinging tightly to his neck. 'I'm just fine.'

'You're shaking.' She felt him move to wrap the edges of his cloak around her. 'Are you cold?'

'No,' Nicola said joyfully into his shoulder. 'I'm laughing.'

She was, too. Laughing with relief and wonder. That she could plunge through the air, convinced that she was about to meet her death, and fall, instead, into the arms of Nathaniel Sheridan, seemed more than simply miraculous. It seemed to Nicola to be the most fantastic thing that had ever happened in the history of the world.

'Is she all right, Nat?' Nicola heard a familiar voice ask, and she looked up to see Nathaniel's father, Lord Sheridan, peering at her from atop his own horse, his expression very worried and kind.

'I'm fine, my lord,' Nicola assured him through tears of mirth and joy.

Lord Sheridan, however, did not seem to share her good humour. He said to his son, 'Get her home. We'll clean up here.'

It was only then that Nicola lifted her head far enough from Nathaniel's shoulder to see what was happening around her. Grant, the cab driver, she soon saw, had met with the same

198

kind of luck she had – only his landing had not, perhaps, been quite so fortuitous, as he had fallen, rear end first, into a water trough. Even as Nicola watched, two Bow Street Runners were struggling to subdue him as he floundered in the trough, spraying plumes of water everywhere, to the amusement of the crowd of rather rough-looking sailors and other individuals who'd gathered around to watch the fun.

From inside the taproom – the Gilded Rose, Nicola saw it was called, at least according to a weather-beaten sign hanging above the door – came the sounds of a struggle. Other Runners were busy rounding up Lord Farelly and the Grouser. 'Unhand me!' Nicola heard Lord Renshaw bleat. 'How dare you? Don't you know I'm a baron?'

Wincing, Lord Sheridan waved at his son. 'Go on,' he called. 'Take Nicola to safety. I believe we'll manage this lot. I'll see you both at home.'

And so Nathaniel, with a nod to his father, turned his horse around and began the long ride back to Mayfair, Nicola in his arms.

Rather, Nicola could not help thinking, the way the brave Lochinvar had carried his fair Ellen upon his rescue of her from her captors.

Much might have been said during the course of such a journey. Tender words and even tenderer caresses might have been exchanged. It would hardly be surprising to learn that Nicola, her arms still clasped firmly around Nathaniel's neck – she would not have loosed them for the world – and her body curled against his in the saddle, completely expected that words of tenderest meaning were shortly to be uttered. Her heart was that full of love and appreciation for all that he'd done for her. For hadn't he, at the risk of his own life, saved hers? Was that not a sign of a genuine and long-lasting affection?

An affection that was more than returned. Nicola was now prepared to admit what for months – perhaps even years – she'd suspected she'd known, but never quite been willing to accept until now: that she loved Nathaniel Sheridan. That she had been in love with him for ages. And that no other man would ever make her happy.

Why else, she asked herself, should he have driven her so mad with his teasing? Why else had his refusal to read the books she loved always enraged her so? And why else was it that now that she had a rather close-up look of that single lock of hair that was forever falling over his eyes, she was completely convinced that she loved that lock more dearly than she had ever loved anything before in her life?

No, there was no help for it. She loved Nathaniel Sheridan – the real Nathaniel Sheridan, not some godlike dream of him she'd made up inside her head – more than she had ever loved anyone she had ever known.

And so it was no little shock when Nathaniel's first words to her as they made their way home were not protestations of his own undying affection for her, but, rather, a rebuke.

'What were you thinking,' he demanded, sounding genuinely annoyed, 'leaving the house like that without telling anyone where you were going?'

Nicola, lifting her head from his shoulder, looked up at him astonishedly. Where was the marriage proposal she'd been expecting? Where were the sweet words of devotion, protestations of undying love and affection?

And what did he mean, blaming *her* for what had happened?

'That wasn't my fault,' she cried. 'They tricked me!'

'Harold Blenkenship told us all about how they tricked you,' Nathaniel informed her – quite angrily, she thought. 'Only an utter fool would have fallen for such a trick.

200

Sir Hugh, asking you to meet him at Grafton House. The idea! He never would have done such a thing in a thousand years.'

Nicola, beginning to feel a good deal less loving toward him, and a good deal nettled instead, loosened her hold on his neck somewhat.

'The note said it was to be a surprise,' she said defensively. 'A surprise for Eleanor. How was I to know it was all a lie?'

'Because if you had the sense God gave a cat,' Nathaniel retorted, 'you'd know Sir Hugh is too much of a gentleman ever to ask an unmarried lady to meet him alone, even in the middle of the day, and in a public place. Nicola, it's a wonder you weren't killed. You very easily could have been, you know.'

Nicola felt all the giddy laughter that had been welling up inside her ebb away. Now all she felt was sadness. Nathaniel did not return her ardour. How could he, and still speak to her so cruelly? Didn't he know he was ruining what could have been a very beautiful moment?

'I know that now,' she said, trying very hard not to sniffle. She was so disappointed! 'But you needn't be so awful about it. It was a simple mistake.'

'A mistake that could have cost you your life!' Nathaniel cried as he steered his horse through the narrow streets . . . which were starting to become wider, the houses on either side of them less dilapidated as they moved farther into the heart of the city. 'I swear, Nicola, sometimes I think you need a keeper.'

She had to blink back tears. He had never called her by her full name so many times in a row. Usually it was Nicky, or sometimes Nick. But never Nicola. Her full name sounded very ominous coming from Nathaniel Sheridan's lips.

It was clear now that he didn't love her after all. Perhaps he never had. Perhaps all of that teasing had simply been banter between friends. Perhaps it had not, after all, been to mask any deeper, stronger emotion, as she'd sometimes suspected.

Oh, all right. Hoped.

'Well,' she said, unable to keep from sniffling now, but trying to disguise it as a cough. 'At least I did the right thing in the end. I convinced Harold to go for help.'

'If that's not an example of the blind leading the blind, I don't know what is.' Nathaniel sounded thoroughly disgusted now. 'If that boy escapes a thrashing from me, it's only because I was too busy getting you out of the mess he's partly responsible for getting you into in the first place. If he had just said something from the beginning—'

'He did,' Nicola said, a little astounded to find she was coming to the Milksop's defence. 'He tried. You don't understand. It isn't easy for Harold. He wants to be a clothing designer, only his father won't let him.'

'And that makes it all right for him to stand by while innocent girls are being terrorized?' Nathaniel shook his head, his profile looking very grim and stern in the light from the gas lamp burning on the street corner. He did not look at all inclined to kiss her, as Nicola had rather been hoping he might. 'I tell you, Nicky. There's going to be hell to pay for all this. Your uncle's going to jail, and I wouldn't be too surprised to see Lord Farelly and the viscount clapped in irons, as well.'

'He isn't my uncle,' Nicola said without thinking.

Then, suddenly, it struck her that he had called her Nicky. No, really, he had! She was sure of it.

Which meant perhaps there was hope, after all.

Only Nicola would have to, she knew, go very carefully indeed. Accordingly, she tightened her grip on his neck just the tiniest bit.

202

'In any case,' she said hesitantly, anxious not to set him off again, 'you came just in time, Nat. Just like . . . just like Lochinvar!'

She had momentarily forgotten, of course, idiot girl that she was, the depths of his disgust for that noble knight. But she was instantly reminded of it when he turned his head and looked down at her with a frown.

'Oh, Nat!' Nicola cried, instantly crushed. 'Really. You simply must get over this absurd prejudice you have against poetry. Whatever is wrong with it, anyway?'

As his horse made its slow but steady way down the city streets, Nathaniel, oblivious to the many curious looks they were getting – it was odd indeed to see a handsome young man with a pretty girl, quite without a bonnet and gloves, and missing a shoe, slung across his saddle like a prize won in battle – admitted, with a shrug, 'It's just all so stupid. No one talks that way, Nicky. Not in real life. Why can't they say it plainer, the way people talk? That's why I don't like it. I don't – I can't, really – understand it.' Then, with renewed anger, he said, 'Why can't Romeo, instead of saying all those bits about wishing he were a glove, just come out and say he loves her?'

Nicola, unable to help herself, loosed one of her hands from around his neck and reached up to stroke the loose lock of hair that had fallen across his forehead. She didn't want to do it. She simply couldn't stop.

'Because then the play would be too short,' she said. 'And no one would think they'd got their money's worth.'

Nathaniel, if he noticed what she was doing to his hair, did not appear to care. Instead he said fiercely, 'I suppose that's how Bartholomew got you to agree to marry him. He flung a lot of poetry at you.'

'Actually,' Nicola said, 'he didn't. He didn't have to. You

see, I didn't even know Lord Sebastian. I said yes when he asked me to marry him because I loved – or thought I loved – an idea I had of him. But my idea of him was totally wrong from the reality of him. You tried to warn me so, but I wouldn't listen.'

'I'll say.'

Suddenly Nathaniel hauled on the reins of his horse, until they were stopped in the middle of the street. Now even more people than ever were looking at them, but Nathaniel did not appear to notice. The arm he'd curled about her – the one keeping her upright in the saddle – tightened, and he said, looking very intently down into her face, 'Wait a minute, Nick. Do you mean to say . . . Do you mean to say you don't love Bartholomew anymore?'

'No,' Nicola said, dropping her hand from his hair and circling his neck with both arms instead. 'I mean to say I never loved him in the first place. I only thought I did, because it was easier than admitting to myself the truth about who I *really* loved.'

'And who,' Nathaniel asked very pointedly, as if her answer mattered to him a great deal, 'is that?'

Nicola looked away from him, but couldn't keep a flirtatious little smile from creeping across her face.

'My goodness,' she said. 'For someone who got a first in mathematics from Oxford, your powers of deduction aren't very strong at all, are they?'

For a moment Nathaniel only looked down at her in confusion. Then an expression of heartfelt delight spread across his face. A second later he was crushing Nicola to him in an embrace that was every bit as possessive as it was affectionate.

'Nicky!' he said joyfully into her dishevelled hair. 'Do you mean it? Or are you only teasing?'

Nicola pulled away from him a little – a difficult feat, given the strength of the arms that held her – so that she could look up into his face.

'Of course I'm not teasing,' she said, as seriously as she had ever said anything in her life. 'I tried to put it plainly, so you could understand. I know how you feel about poetry—'

But she wasn't allowed to say anything more. That was because Nathaniel's lips, coming down over hers, silenced her for the moment.

And Nicola, who'd been kissed before only by a god, realized that being kissed by a mortal was a great deal more satisfying, because he seemed really to mean it. Or maybe it was only because this time she was being kissed by a man she truly loved, and whose friendship she valued above all others . . .

In any case, being kissed by Nathaniel Sheridan, even on the back of a horse in the middle of a public street, was quite the most exciting thing that had ever happened to Nicola.

At least until Nathaniel lifted his head to say, in a raw voice, 'Nicky, I love you so,' and then proceeded to kiss her even more deeply.

And really *that*, Nicola decided, was the most exciting thing that had ever happened to her. At least until he said it again.

Twenty

'Well, Nana,' Nicola said, as she plucked a piece of ginger cake from its plate and popped it into her mouth, forgetting, for the moment, Madame's warning against speaking with one's mouth full. 'What do you think of him?'

Nana looked up from the pitcher of lemonade she was preparing – from lemons supplied by Lady Sheridan's seafaring brother – with a broad smile on her plump face.

'Oh, Miss Nicky,' she said, her blue eyes glittering. 'He's a rum 'un, that one. Ye couldn't've picked better if ye'd've held a husband contest.'

'Yes,' Nicola said with some satisfaction. 'I think so, too. And Puddy? Does Puddy like him?'

'Why, of course he does!' The old woman, the closest thing Nicola had ever known to a grandmother, crinkled her eyes merrily. 'Your young man's already shown 'im a better way to figure out the accounts from the milk and the sheep's wool.'

'Nathaniel's quite good with numbers,' Nicola said.

'He's a fine young man,' Nana informed her approvingly. 'You've done well, Miss Nicky.'

Nicola could not help agreeing. She *had* done well. More than well, as a matter of fact. She was quite the luckiest girl in the world . . . something Eleanor appeared only too eager to concede when Nicola, a few moments later, found her at the picnic blanket they'd spread across the abbey lawn.

'Oh, Nicky.' Eleanor sighed, looking up at the cloudless blue sky above them. 'You're so lucky.'

Nicola, refilling her friend's cup from the pitcher Nana had provided her, followed her gaze. The summer sky really was a stunning shade of azure. One couldn't see a single sign of the clouds of smoke from the colliery ten miles away.

'Because I'm an orphan?' Nicola asked.

'No, not because of that.' Eleanor sat up. 'Because of all this.' She threw out an arm, seeming to wish to encompass the green pasture all around them, the arc of blue above them, and the quaint manor house behind them all in one gesture. 'It's so beautiful!'

'And to think,' Nicola said, lying down on the blanket beside her friend. 'They were going to put a train through it.'

'I'm so glad you didn't let them,' Eleanor said seriously. 'I mean, I am all for progress, Nicky, but not—'

'—when it's going straight through your parlour,' Nicola finished for her. 'I know. I feel the same way. Stockton and Darlington can build all the railways they want, so long as they don't do so on *my* property.'

'At least they apologized,' Eleanor reminded her. 'I mean, Mr Pease didn't know you were opposed to selling. Lord Renshaw told him you'd be delighted to part with the abbey.'

'I think the Grouser's learned the error of his ways,' Nicola said, rolling over onto her stomach and reaching for a nearby daisy. 'Don't you?'

'Considering he's currently residing in Newgate Prison, you mean?' Eleanor let out a gentle laugh. 'Yes, I think so. I hope he and Lord Farelly are enjoying their new accommodations.'

'And Lord Sebastian,' Nicola said, plucking a petal from

the daisy she'd picked. *He loves me.* 'Don't forget Lord Sebastian.'

'Oh, Lord Sebastian.' Eleanor lay down beside her friend, resting her chin in one hand. 'How could I forget? Still, it seems a shame, all that manly beauty locked up in a prison cell.'

'He ought to have thought about that,' Nicola said, plucking another petal, 'before he agreed to go along with his father's scheme.' *He loves me not.*

'Without a doubt. And did I tell you, Nick? Lady Farelly's had to decamp for the Continent, she's become so unpopular because of all this. Not a soul in London would have her in their home, after the papers got hold of what her husband had tried to do to you.'

'Better the Continent,' Nicola said, 'than prison.' *He loves me.*

'True. But, oh, Nicky! I very nearly forgot. I heard the strangest thing just before we left. Lady Honoria! What do you think? They say she ran off to America. *America*, of all places, Nicky! And you'll never guess with whom.'

'Oh, I think I can guess,' Nicola said. *He loves me not.* 'My cousin Harold?'

Eleanor let out a little shriek. 'Yes! Isn't it the strangest thing you've ever heard? Lady Honoria and the Milksop! I can't imagine how he talked her into doing it . . . though I don't suppose it was probably very hard, given the alternative. Certainly, like her mother, she was done in London. But still. To choose the Milksop over one's own mother – she must really have hated Lady Farelly. Why, I thought I should never stop laughing when I heard it.'

'I think it's a good thing,' Nicola said. 'So long as he keeps her away from feathers.' *He loves me.*

'Where do you think the others have gone off to?' Eleanor sat up again and, shading her eyes, peered off into the distance. 'Oh, Lord, Nicky. You'll never guess what Hugh and Nat are up to now.'

He loves me not. 'You're right. I couldn't guess. What are they up to?'

'Well, they're rather far away . . . but I think . . . Lord, Nicky, I think they're teaching Phillip to swim.'

Nicola sat up at once and followed her friend's gaze. 'Are they naked?'

'No,' was Eleanor's disappointing answer. 'Still, I hope Mama can't see them from the house. You know Phil's supposed to be being punished for slipping those duck eggs into the henhouse.'

Nicola had rather found the sight of so many ducklings straggling after a very confused-looking chicken secretly amusing, but had not admitted so in front of her guests, Lord and Lady Sheridan, who'd been furious with their youngest son.

'Two years,' Eleanor murmured, still gazing toward the stream. 'It seems ages, doesn't it? I think it quite unfair of Mama to make you and Nat wait so long, as well. It isn't as if you're her daughter.'

Nicola, turning back to her daisy, shrugged. Like Phil's trick with the duck eggs, Nicola secretly liked Lady Sheridan's mandate that Nathaniel and she wait to marry until she'd turned eighteen. Having never had a mother of her own, Nicola rather enjoyed having Lady Sheridan boss her about. It was like being back at Madame Vieuxvincent's . . . except with the added bonus of being kissed, soundly and often, by the man she loved. *He loves me.*

Suddenly Eleanor reached out and grabbed one of the monogrammed tea towels in which their picnic luncheon had been wrapped.

'Why, Nicky!' she cried. 'I'd completely forgotten till now.

But how delightful! Your initials aren't going to change. Nicola Sparks. Nicola Sheridan. Why, you don't even have to have new towels made.'

'Yes,' Nicola said in a pleased voice. 'I know.' *He loves me not.*

'And did you ever think that when Papa dies, Nat will become viscount in his place?' Eleanor wanted to know. 'So in the end, Nicky, you're going to be a viscountess after all. Really.' Eleanor shook her head until her brown curls swayed. 'But you simply have to be the luckiest girl alive!'

'Yes, I am, aren't I?' Nicola mused.

She looked up as she heard Nathaniel, coming toward them, call her name. The stray lock of hair that was always falling into his eyes was plastered wetly to his forehead.

'Nicky,' he called. 'Come on. The water's perfect!'

He loves me.

The PRINCESS DIARIES Princess Club

HEY, PRINCESS,

WANNA JOIN THE PRINCESS DIARIES PRINCESS CLUB?

4 fantastic comps and regular
doses of fashion, gossip and games direct
2 ur mobile txt ur date of birth (dd,mm,yy)

to **07950 080700**

You will also get FREE
unpublished snippets, exclusive
games & comps!